"Don't you ever wear any clothes?"

His eyes traced the curve of her lashes, her cheekbones, her mouth, before dropping to linger below.

"This is a perfectly respectable outfit for working out," Sidney defended. She'd never been subjected to such unqualified male approval at such close quarters.

"Don't get me wrong," Beau said. "I'm not complaining."

"Please don't do that," Sidney objected.

"Am I staring?" He laughed ruefully. "You're really something, Miss Sidney James, you know that?" Briefly, he allowed himself one appreciative assessment of her. "And I love your outfit."

Sidney forced herself to withstand the sensual assault of his eyes.

"Maybe I can change your mind," he said, looking like a big, tawny tomcat.

Sidney made a small sound of protest.

"I'm going to work on it."

No, not a tomcat. A jungle cat.

Dear Reader,

Although our culture is always changing, the desire to love and be loved is a constant in every woman's heart. Silhouette Romances reflect that desire, sweeping you away with books that will make you laugh and cry, poignant stories that will move you time and time again.

This year we're featuring Romances with a playful twist. Remember those fun-loving heroines who always manage to get themselves into tricky predicaments? You'll enjoy reading about their escapades in Silhouette Romances by Brittany Young, Debbie Macomber, Annette Broadrick and Rita Rainville.

We're also publishing Romances by many of your all-time favorites such as Ginna Gray, Diana Palmer and Joan Hohl. Your overwhelming reaction to these authors has served as a touchstone for us, and we're pleased to bring you more books with Silhouette's distinctive medley of charm, wit and—above all—*romance*. I hope you enjoy this book, and the many stories to come.

Sincerely,

Rosalind Noonan
Senior Editor
SILHOUETTE BOOKS

KAREN YOUNG
Darling Detective

Silhouette Romance

Published by Silhouette Books New York

America's Publisher of Contemporary Romance

For my mother
who is everthing a mother should be.

SILHOUETTE BOOKS
300 E. 42nd St., New York, N.Y. 10017

Copyright © 1986 by Karen Stone

ISBN: 0-373-08433-1

First Silhouette Books printing May 1986
Second printing July 1986

America's Publisher of Contemporary Romance

Printed in the U.S.A.

Books by Karen Young

Silhouette Romance

Yesterday's Promise #212
Irresistible Intruder #284
A Wilder Passion #380
Darling Detective #433

KAREN YOUNG

and her husband, Paul, have moved eighteen times during twenty-five years of marriage. Because of their mobile life-style, Karen has observed many different types of people and has included them in her plots.

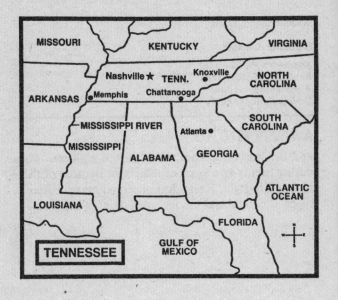

Prologue

Be reasonable, Beau. What do you care if an accountant takes a corner of an office in your plant? I give you my word you will not be harassed.''

Beau Rutledge surged up out of his chair, frustration in every line of his lean frame. He stared blindly through the window of the Peabody Bank, reminding himself that he didn't have a lot of options. He was at the bank for the express purpose of getting a loan.

"It's a stipulation tacked on by the board, I'm afraid," Louis Maynard was saying in a mildly apologetic tone. "We have a high-risk situation here, Beau, and the bank's own interests are best served if progress is monitored on a daily basis."

Beau leaned an elbow against the window frame, his expression bitter. "You mean monitored by a spy who will nose around, second-guess all my decisions and generally make my life a misery." His voice was laced with outrage.

When the bank official didn't respond, Beau pushed away from the window. "Give me a break, Louis! You've got my land as collateral! I lose everything if I don't make it work. That's all the incentive I need to use the funds judiciously." He paced restlessly, his long legs eating up the length of the plush office.

"Can I get you a drink, Beau?"

Beau laughed shortly. "No thanks, Louis. Nine in the morning is a little early, even for me," he replied dryly, sprawling with natural grace into the depths of a leather chair.

"I never believed you were half as reckless as folks made out," Louis replied sagely, to Beau's amazement. He'd always assumed that his father's opinion had been shared by everyone in Memphis, especially those of his father's generation. Beau and John Rutledge had been too much alike to live together peaceably. Working together had been impossible. The tension in Beau eased slightly. Louis's quiet voice of confidence soothed his raw emotions.

Louis leaned back and studied the younger man candidly. "I'm glad you're back in town, Beau, glad you've taken the reins at Rutledge Enterprises. John, God rest his soul, wouldn't believe the economy today, would he?"

Still struggling with the objectionable nature of his errand, Beau made an effort to follow the banker's stream of family reminiscences and local gossip as Louis continued, "How's your mama, son? And your little niece, Megan? Pretty as a picture, that one. So young to lose both Ben and Alicia. Drunk drivers are a hazard on the roads, that's for certain."

The older man shook his head sadly over the tragedy of Beau's brother and sister-in-law before shuffling through a thick file on his desk. He peered keenly through his bifocals at what looked to Beau like a computer printout balance sheet.

"I guess you've had a chance to study the status of Rutledge now that Ben's and Alicia's wills have been probated," Louis stated, his blue eyes questioning Beau over the rim of his bifocals.

Beau nodded curtly.

"Ben had full control," the banker said. "In fact, he'd been acting with full power of attorney since John's first stroke."

Beau met Louis's look directly. "Yeah, I think I've got the picture. When the mills reached a production low, apparently Ben borrowed from Vince Trehern, putting up shares in Rutledge as collateral. Unfortunately, the number three mill is producing at only forty-five percent of maximum. The other two are holding. It will take seventy-five percent steady production to operate profitably. If that doesn't happen, Vince is sure to seize his shares." Beau moved his chair forward, his tone grim. "My father would literally come back and haunt me if the company passed out of the Rutledge family, Louis."

"Even so, it wouldn't be your doing, Beau," Louis pointed out reasonably. "Ben's the one who went into business with Trehern."

Beau's gaze drifted to some vague point beyond Louis. "It's my responsibility to see that nothing comes of it, no matter who did it."

Louis nodded, looking gratified in a way that puzzled Beau, but before he could figure it out, Louis said, "You're in a precarious situation here, Beau. You're going to have to manage carefully and have the luck of the devil besides to pull out of this."

Beau was silent. No one knew better than he what a task he had.

"I want to remind you of the possibility of disaster to you personally, as a Rutledge, if you fail."

"I'm aware of the consequences, Louis."

"You'd lose everything, Beau."

"I know."

"John wouldn't approve."

"My father's dead."

Louis looked pained. "Yes, that's so."

Beau uncoiled from the chair, unable to sit still a second longer. He gazed out over downtown Memphis. "So, using both tracts of Rutledge prime land, the bank will approve the loan?"

"With the stipulation we discussed," Louis replied.

Beau turned. "Your resident accountant," he said sardonically. "I haven't forgotten."

Louis waved a placating hand. "To furnish reports, inspections on demand, that kind of thing, Beau. You can understand the board's reservations."

Beau took a deep breath and expressed his thanks with grim fortitude. But a hard determined look made his eyes gleam like topaz.

The banker nodded graciously, while silently acknowledging the astonishing likeness between the late John Rutledge and Beau. Louis was counting on Beau's having inherited more than looks from his father. John Rutledge's shrewdness would be a gift worth more than gold. A tiny frown flicked across Louis's features. Something just didn't seem right at Rutledge, but he couldn't put his finger on it. He was betting Beau would figure it out. In fact, Louis was counting on it. The board would have his shirt if he was wrong.

"Oh, one more thing," Louis said, halting Beau at the door. "Every year we have a little summer fete at the country club and tomorrow's the night for this year. Wouldn't hurt for you to be there. The board's a bunch of rascals, but they're human, too. If you present yourself well, show 'em you've got the same Rutledge blood that ran in John's veins, I guarantee they'll roll over and play dead for you, Beau."

Beau left, shaking his head helplessly. In spite if himself, his sense of humor stirred. It was difficult to see the Peabody's board of directors fall victim to his questionable charisma. But it was worth a try.

Chapter One

"You're going to be working with *who* starting Monday?" Jill squeaked.

Sidney James rolled her eyes heavenward, not missing the note of unmitigated delight in her friend's voice. "Whom," she said tersely, striding across the lawn toward her VW Rabbit. She yanked open the door and tossed her tote bag onto the back seat.

"Okay, whom," Jill returned agreeably, scrambling into the passenger seat and buckling up. "You're going to work with that gorgeous hunk, Beau Rutledge—that's a quote—and it's all in the line of duty? Now have I got it right?"

"I'm not sure about the gorgeous hunk part," Sidney returned dryly, "but the duty part is right."

Jill Sinclair's grin broadened as Sidney started the car and backed out of the driveway with something less than her usual finesse. Jill shook her head helplessly, her dark curls bobbing. "Ah, Sidney, Megan's going to love this. She's just going to *love* this!"

Sidney smothered a sigh. "Tell me about it."

"And to think it happened without Megan lifting a finger," Jill marveled wickedly. "She's probably going to be disappointed that you and Beau are finally going to meet without her personally arranging it. For weeks now she's thrown all of her sixteen-year-old ingenuity into making a match between you and her darling uncle!"

"Sometimes, Jill, you seem as bad as Megan," Sidney muttered, doggedly maneuvering the little car through the maze of parked vehicles before turning into the traffic heading toward downtown Memphis.

"It's fate, that's what," Jill stated firmly. "Kismet." She darted a mischievous look at Sidney. "Maybe Megan has something, Sid. After all, Beau is highly eligible. He's the heir to the Rutledge dynasty, or what's left of it anyway. Granted, we haven't seen him yet, but how ugly can he be?"

"Jill!"

Jill laughed and settled back for a minute, but Sidney's hopes of quelling the irrepressible brunette's questions were soon dashed. "I know the confidential nature of your work and all that, Sid, but you've just got to tell me how this came about."

Sidney eased into the fast lane of the parkway and accelerated. "It's simple, really," she explained. "Rutledge Enterprises has been a client of the Peabody Bank practically forever. When Megan Rutledge's parents were killed three months ago, J. R. Rutledge—or Beau as he's known in Memphis—came home from Atlanta and picked up the reins of the business."

That was true as far as it went but, as Jill said, there were other details Sidney couldn't reveal, such as the fact that Rutledge Enterprises was perilously close to bankruptcy, and that Louis Maynard, Sidney's boss and president of the Peabody, had gone out on a limb and approved a sizable loan to Rutledge even though he was suspicious of some of the company's past transactions. Why? Sidney wondered, especially since Louis had confided that Rutledge's assets didn't produce the profit margin he believed they should. "The secret's in the numbers, Sidney," Louis had stated confidently. "I want you to find it."

"My job will be to keep track of the bank's interests at Rutledge Enterprises," Sidney told Jill. "But I'll admit that I was stunned when Louis told me that I'll be at the plant itself for the duration of the bank's transactions with Rutledge."

Jill looked bemused for a moment. "And to think I always believed accountants led a dull life."

Sidney laughed. "Look who's talking. Compared to a lady who operates her own fitness center, coaches a gymnastics team and is a single parent to boot, accounting is pretty tame."

"Hah! Can we get serious here? How many accountants do I know—lady accountants, that is—who've had a career as a private detective?"

Sidney's expression was pained. "Oh, Jill, not that again! How many times do I have to tell you that the job in Atlanta wasn't as sensational as you think."

"Stakeouts, surveillance and marital hanky-panky is sensational, lady." And before Sidney could argue, Jill continued, "I know, I know, that's all behind you now. You're just a staid efficient employee of the straitlaced Peabody Bank."

"Exactly."

"Of course, sometimes that mundane existence can be livened up by an assignment such as the Rutledge caper."

"Jill!"

Chuckling, Jill pulled out her clipboard to look over the choreography for an aerobics exercise while Sidney jostled for space on the expressway. Though Sidney tried to keep her mind on the clutch of traffic, her thoughts kept veering along a different course. A direction that they'd persistently taken since Louis dropped his bomb yesterday.

As the Peabody's ace financial detective, Sidney was going to be assigned to the Rutledge plant whether she liked it or not. And ordinarily she would be eager to accept the assignment. It was just her cup of tea. But not when it involved Beau Rutledge.

Sidney knew this case was going to be trouble. Although Jill, Megan and everybody else in Memphis thought Rutledge was a stranger to her, Sidney knew better.

Sidney hadn't been an accountant two years ago; she'd been a private detective and Rutledge her quarry. His wife, Lisa, had retained the Thompson Agency to prove her suspicions about her husband's extramarital activities. Sidney herself had photographed Rutledge with his secretary in a couple of situations usually described in the divorce court as "compromising." Although Sidney hadn't been completely satisfied with the evidence since everything to that point had been strictly circumstantial, Lisa Rutledge had seemed convinced. She had collected the photographs, paid the agency and canceled the contract.

Sidney's green eyes were puzzled as she gazed over the bulk of a van. She found herself wishing she'd had a little more time on the case. The limited access she'd had to the Rutledge business had only whetted her appetite. She suspected someone had tampered with the computer, and she had been very close to zeroing in on exactly how the culprit was doing it. But Lisa Rutledge had inexplicably called a halt to all investigations. Sidney never knew why. As it was, all she had was a lot of loose ends. Sidney hated loose ends.

"Where are all these people going on a Saturday morning?" Jill wondered idly, breaking into Sidney's thoughts. "Wherever they're going, at least they have transportation, which is more than I have. I've *got* to get a new battery."

Sidney flashed her friend a quick smile. "You know you're welcome to catch a ride with me anytime, Jill. How's Josh this morning?"

"As terrible as two-year-olds are reputed to be. He woke me up at six demanding his breakfast. I can't figure out how he's getting out of that crib!"

"Maybe he's working on becoming a gymnast like his mom," Sidney said with a smile, visualizing Jill's lively son. Jill was a single parent. Every day was a struggle to pick up the pieces of her life. Jill's Place, a fitness center, was the direct result of a lot of hard work and dogged determination to make it without Mike Sinclair. Jill's problems only added to Sidney's conviction that marriage was a gamble that more people lost than won. It tended to make one shy away from commitment.

"Anyway," Jill went on cheerfully, "I managed to put Josh off a full five minutes, then gave it up when he found some stale crackers and tried to stuff them in my mouth. He's a lot better than an alarm clock.''

"But he's adorable and you love it."

Jill chuckled. "Yeah, he's adorable, if I do say so."

"My opinion too, Mom."

Jill tilted her head and eyed Sidney knowingly. "You'd make a wonderful mother, Sid. Josh adores you, you seem so natural around kids. You ought to—''

"Don't start, Jill..." Sidney began in a warning tone, although her smile lingered.

"Well, it's true. You meet dozens of men in your work, but no one ever seems to catch your fancy."

"I'm perfectly satisfied with my social life, Jill. As a matter of fact, I had dinner with Ted Lipscomb last night and I had a lovely time."

"What color are his eyes?"

Sidney flicked a startled glance at Jill. "What?"

Patiently, Jill repeated, "What color are his eyes?"

Amused and a little exasperated, Sidney said, "Gray, I think, or light brown.... Mmm, yes, that's it—brown. I think."

"You see!" Jill exclaimed. "When you spend the evening with a man and don't even notice what color his eyes are, there's something missing, my friend."

"The light was bad."

"Some people call that romantic."

"I could hardly tell if my filet was done enough!"

Jill's patience was exhausted. "If the feeling was there, you wouldn't care!"

Sidney sent a sly look at her exasperated friend. "Well, I could have gone out with Spencer, but—"

"Spencer Foley! I'll never understand what you ever saw in him."

"I don't have to have a man around to make my life complete, Jill," Sidney stated firmly.

"Apparently not," Jill agreed disgustedly. "Because Spencer Foley doesn't conjure up any particularly masculine fantasies."

"Come on, Jill. Spencer is a very nice man."

"Sid, if you look in the dictionary under dull and boring," said Jill patiently, "it says Spencer Foley."

Sidney choked a giggle, determined not to encourage Jill. "He's kind, considerate, well educated, he's... eligible, for heaven's sake. Aren't those all the attributes you've been nagging me about?"

Jill's look said exactly how she felt about Spencer Foley, no matter how many sterling qualities he possessed. And deep down, Sidney was inclined to agree. Spencer was a salesman she'd met while she lived in Atlanta. They'd drifted into a comfortable kind of relationship, but when she moved to Memphis she'd left him behind as easily as she'd left her job. A few weeks ago, Memphis had been added to his sales territory and he'd appeared, ready to resume their friendship. But Sidney had been unenthusiastic.

Spencer was everything she'd told Jill he was, but he was also ultraconservative, always keenly aware of the appearance of things. And people. The few times he'd glimpsed that wayward little quirk in Sidney that sometimes compelled her to do something out of the ordinary, he'd been extremely cool. Definitely disapproving. He'd viewed her job as a private detective as unsuitable for a young woman with her educational background.

Sidney sighed somewhat wistfully. Where was the exciting attractive man who would be willing to let a woman develop all the facets of her personality and still love her totally? Did such a person exist?

"I know that sigh wasn't brought on by thoughts of Spencer," Jill observed dryly.

Sidney flicked on the turn signal to exit. "Can we change the subject?"

Jill glanced around blankly. "Where are we going?"

"I left a package in my desk yesterday and I want to go by the bank and pick it up. The Peabody's summer fete is tomorrow night and I bought an antique ivory comb to wear in my hair."

Jill eyed the dark russet mane and sighed enviously. "It'll look wonderful. Is Rutledge invited?"

Sidney nodded, looking resigned. "Louis plans to introduce us then. Louis is convinced that he can persuade Rutledge to accept having me on his territory, but from Megan's remarks about her uncle, Rutledge doesn't strike me as a man who will appreciate anybody poking around the family corporation." *Bank loan or no bank loan,* she added silently.

But some wary instinct urged Sidney to steer clear of Rutledge. Not that she feared any hostility from him. Actually, they'd never even met. The Thompson Agency had been discreet. Sidney and Lisa Rutledge had conducted their business privately and, as far as Sidney knew, the man had never been the wiser. But Sidney had left the agency and Atlanta before the Rutledge file had been closed. The practical efficient part of her wished for black and white proof of his guilt. Or innocence. Was he a man whose marriage vows meant nothing to him? Was he guilty of unethical business practices?

It was not only Saturday morning traffic that had Sidney agitated as she prepared to exit the expressway.

She had this eerie feeling that Rutledge was going to be nothing but trouble. It was bad enough that she was forced to work right alongside him. She could just imagine the complications that would follow if he learned that she'd had a hand, however unintentionally, in his divorce. It could be awkward, to say the least. She pressed a hand against a fluttery stomach. Why the devil did it have to be him of all people!

She pulled into the Peabody's parking lot and quickly pushed open the door of the Rabbit. "I'll just be a second, Jill." She looked down at her workout shorts and cutoff T-shirt ruefully. "My 'staid' image will be destroyed if anybody sees me this way. It's early, though, so only the guard will be around, I hope."

Jill waved a careless hand and pulled her clipboard on top of her knees. "Take your time. I'm going to go over a new dance routine while I've got a minute."

The guard recognized Sidney and obligingly unlocked the door. "Morning, James," she said with a smile, slipping inside the cool foyer of the Peabody. Her office was on the mezzanine level overlooking the lobby. Instead of using the elevator, she ran quickly up the curving stairs to her office and pulled the package from the bottom drawer of her desk. At the sound of voices from Louis's office next door, she hastily pushed the drawer closed, flicked off the lights and dashed for the stairs.

She was more than halfway down when the package slipped from her fingers. "Darn!" she muttered, turning to pick it up. A man's deep tones drew her gaze in the direction of Louis's office.

That was when she saw him.

She froze, eyes intent on the large male silhouetted against the light from Louis's doorway. It was Rutledge. She'd know the set of those shoulders, the angle of that tawny head anywhere. Hadn't she observed him for weeks on end two years ago?

Straightening slowly, she assessed his familiar loose-limbed grace, acknowledging an equally familiar response that the sight of him always evoked. *So much for Jill's observation that no man ever captures my fancy,* Sidney thought tersely. Sheer feminine appreciation bloomed within her. He *was* an attractive devil.

Even after all the weeks of surveillance she'd devoted to him, she'd never been able to stifle a purely feminine response to the sight of Rutledge. And that familiar sensual curiosity was stirring again, she realized with dismay, trying to push it away, far into the back of her mind. For a crazy second, she even found herself almost sympathizing with his secretary. He looked like a man who took what he wanted, and if he wanted a woman, it would be difficult to resist him.... With a tiny gasp, she hauled in her wayward thoughts before they became any more ridiculous.

It didn't look as if she was going to be able to avoid a face-to-face encounter, Sidney noted, her stomach clutching in panic. Not unless she resorted to a mad dash down the remaining stairs, and pride forbade that option. Resigned, she watched him shake hands with Louis, observing the grim slant of his mouth and his brows locked in a scowl. There was certainly no trace of the legendary Rutledge charm visible anywhere on his tanned features. She found herself studying the tall broad-shouldered look of him. Tawny hair, thick and shot with gold, was slightly long for her taste, Sidney told herself, but she had to concede grudgingly that it looked right on him, simply adding to his rakish appeal. One arm of his sunglasses was anchored casually in the pocket of his white pullover. Soft jeans hugged every line and sinew of him, intensifying his already blatant masculinity.

He moved quickly toward her, and though she wanted nothing so much as to turn and run, she held her ground. Such a juvenile reaction was silly, she admonished herself. He was just a man!

Their eyes locked and he stopped short on the stairs. Sidney was acutely aware of her own appearance as his eyes swept over her. Around her shoulders her deep russet hair fell in a disheveled tumble haphazardly confined in the black bandanna she'd wrapped around her forehead like a sweatband.

Her green eyes were wide and wary on his. She was blissfully unaware of the appeal of her clear creamy complexion and the tantalizing glimpse of her pale flesh through the mesh knit of her cropped-off T-shirt. Her long shapely legs in brief pink shorts were lightly tanned. Her ankles had a fragile look in white Adidas.

"Good morning to you, too," he drawled, flashing a rakish grin. "I can see some much-needed improvements have been made in the Peabody's dress code."

I'll bet he's famous for that grin, Sidney thought coolly, appraising him as he descended slowly, all the while eyeing her like a hungry tiger. "Good morning," she murmured politely, edging away.

He put his hand out, but didn't touch her. "Hey, wait a minute. Do you work here?"

A tiny flicker of amusement came and went as she glanced down at her attire. "Why would you doubt it?"

He chuckled and leaned negligently against the banister. His gaze, slow and warm with pure male appreciation, wandered over her full bosom to the trim line of her waist, then on to the delicate flare of her hips and back up to her mouth.

The blood in her veins rose in a heated rush at that look.

"Believe me, doing business with the Peabody suddenly seems a lot more promising than it did five minutes ago," he said huskily.

Sidney stared into his eyes, determined not to be bowled over by his lazy charm. "I wouldn't get my hopes up," she retorted tartly. "They're doing business much as they've always done."

He stared fixedly into her eyes as though he couldn't quite believe their color. And then seeing the disapproval there, he frowned. "Is there a message for me somewhere in that fierce look?" he asked, even though his eyes still brimmed with amusement.

What was the matter with her? Of course the Peabody was going to do business with the owner of Rutledge Enterprises. Any questionable behavior this man might have engaged in was apparently unimportant to Louis Maynard. "Excuse me," she murmured, already regretting her retort. Her head came up when he moved to intercept her.

"Are you coming or going?" he inquired, flicking another admiring look at her unlikely outfit.

Topaz. When Jill asked her what color his eyes were, Sidney would have the answer. Up close, he had even broader shoulders than she'd realized. He was taller, too. A full six feet two or three, she judged. And his tan was deeper. With a will of its own, her gaze traveled over his face. His sensual mouth stretched into a lazy smile and Sidney stared, fascinated.

"Which is it?" he asked, his grin telling her he'd been aware of her intense look.

"What?"

"Coming or going," he supplied with a look at the dark fire of her hair. Unconsciously, he reached out a hand, but before he could touch the errant strand that had escaped the rolled band, she shied away, flashing him a wary look.

"Going," she told him, tucking the vibrant tendril firmly in place. "Have a nice day."

"What would make it really nice is having lunch with you." He grinned disarmingly, pressing with typical male tenacity, "What do you say?"

"I say no," she replied, ". . . thank you."

He studied her for a second, his head tipped to one side. "No problem," he said lazily. "We have other options here. How about coffee?"

She sighed impatiently. "Would you let me pass, please?" She turned away, but not before seeing the wicked glint in his eye.

"Lady," he drawled, "I think I should warn you that I don't take rejection very well."

She gave him one last exasperated look and flounced off.

Beau watched with a bemused half smile as she hurried toward the door. Her perfume, something flowery and fresh, lingered to tantalize his senses. It had been a long time since any woman had stirred a response of any kind in him. And he hadn't lied when he'd told her he wasn't used to rejection. He started after her recklessly, hoping she didn't have him cast in the role of mugger or thief or something.

He watched enviously as she flashed James a warm smile, but the look she gave him as he approached the guard to be let out should have warned him off. A mixture of curiosity and male pride pushed him to pursue her anyway. He hadn't been spurned by a woman before and the experience was chastening, to say the least!

A hand went idly for the sunglasses stuck in his shirt pocket. Maybe he was coming on too heavy. But, damn it! she was going to disappear in another minute. On that thought, he quickly caught up with her, noting the VW Rabbit, which was the only other car besides his own Blazer in the parking lot.

"I'm Beau Rutledge," he said to her lowered head, battling frustration. "Look, I didn't mean to overwhelm you back there. It's just that you're so lovely and I was so surprised to see you there that any finesse I might have used flew right out of my head."

If he had hoped to disarm her with boyish honesty, he saw ruefully that it hadn't worked. Her brisk pace never faltered.

"Just tell me if you work here," he persisted, his smile willing her response. "Will I be seeing you again?"

Her green eyes were still wary as she stared at him. Relenting a moment, she said, "Yes, Mr. Rutledge, you'll be seeing me. Probably more than you bargain for." She dropped a discreet look at her watch. "Now, please excuse me, my friend runs a business and it's time to open the doors."

Reluctantly, he watched her turn, his thoughts baffled and intrigued at the same time. She *was* a secretary, apparently. He was glad of that fact. He'd had more than enough of high-powered career women. And for the first time, the thought of Lisa came and went without the usual knife twist. The day was brighter suddenly. Even his errand wasn't quite as galling as it had been minutes before. His grin flashed again.

"Did I mention that I liked your working attire?"

One brow lifted, the look telling him how supremely indifferent she was to what he liked. "I forgot a package." She raised it briefly and started toward her car.

"Hey," he drawled, his mouth slanted appealingly. "You forgot something else."

"Oh?" She looked back, anything but encouraging.

"You forgot to tell me your name."

He heard his name called out just then and instinctively glanced around, frowning as James motioned him back into the bank. Apparently Louis had forgotten something. When he turned back, he knew he'd missed his last opportunity to find out her name.

He was surprised at the depth of his frustration. A dozen unanswered questions clamored in his head. Again he thought how long it had been since he'd felt this compelling urgency toward any woman. He'd forgotten just how delicious that feeling could be. Pure male anticipation flared. A faint smile curved one side of his mouth. He had unfinished business with that lady.

It took all of Sidney's self-control to cross the parking lot at a sedate pace when her instincts urged her to put some distance between herself and Beau Rutledge as fast as possible. In close quarters, he was even more attractive than she'd feared!

This is ridiculous! she lectured herself fiercely, heading for her car. How could an unexpected encounter with a man she didn't even know rattle her like this?

Deep down she knew. Ever since she'd been old enough to remember, she had been subject to these sudden crazy flights of fancy. Her heart sank as she recognized the symptoms. Rutledge appealed to that wayward streak in her. There was no other explanation. She ground her teeth and threw a pleading glance heavenward. Had four years of college and another two years dedicated to a responsible career changed nothing?

Two years of acting logically and—she groaned—staidly hadn't changed her basic nature. She'd fallen victim to these whims too many times in the past not to recognize the signs. How else to explain that time she'd spent the summer vacation as a cocktail waitress in St. Thomas instead of in a training position at E. F. Hutton? And what about the year she'd paid her tuition by teaching the exotic art of belly dancing in an exclusive health spa in Nevada? She tugged glumly at her pink shorts. Every now and then she did one of these wild and crazy things.

That was how she'd come to take the job with the Thompson Agency, for example. She'd earned her degree in accounting. Nothing could be more sensible than that. But to apply it to financial sleuthing was definitely out of the ordinary. That devilish quirk she was plagued with had made her do it. In fact, Jill hadn't been too far off in her assessment of the job.

Yes, it was that capricious streak in her nature that was attracted to Beau Rutledge. But since coming to the Peabody, she'd kept that little streak under strict control. With a firming of her chin, she stalked over to the Rabbit. That was the way it was going to stay!

"Who was that fantastic man?" Jill demanded as soon as Sidney slid behind the wheel.

"I guess you don't mean James," Sidney muttered, backing out too fast.

Jill gave her an exasperated look. "I know James is the guard, you nut. I meant the hunk that James just ushered back inside the Peabody. The one you just came out with.''

''Would you believe you've just seen Megan's uncle?''

If Sidney hadn't left her sense of humor behind in the lobby, she would have enjoyed the comical look on Jill's face.

''You mean—?''

''Beau Rutledge in person.''

Jill's reaction was an unladylike whistle. ''And what a person! Jiminneee, for once Megan didn't exaggerate. What did he say?''

''About what?''

''About anything, for heaven's sake, Sid! What did he say when you told him who you were? You did speak, didn't you?''

Sidney merged into the expressway before answering. It was clear by the spark in Jill's eye that she wouldn't take kindly to Sidney throwing away any God-given opportunities to meet ''a fantastic man.'' ''He introduced himself and mentioned an appointment with Louis.''

A thoughtful Jill reflected on the nonchalance in Sidney's reply before turning her gaze to the teeming traffic. Sidney could almost hear the wheels turning in her friend's nimble brain. Jill was no fool. She sensed Sidney's agitation and was mulling over its significance. Suddenly Sidney was seized by a mischievous impulse.

''Topaz, Jill.''

Puzzled, Jill turned, her mouth quirked in a half smile.

"His eyes are topaz."

Pure satisfaction broadened the smile. "Now we're getting somewhere."

Chapter Two

Sidney swayed dreamily to the sound of a mellow ballad, lost in the spell of the music and her own delight in moving her body to it. Oblivious to the other women in the class, she moved gracefully, senses languid, body fluid, thoughts suspended. Somewhere on the fringe of her mind she heard Jill's voice leading the exercises, but the steps were so familiar that the moves came naturally, effortlessly. Sweeping deeply, she sank to the floor, head bent, arms outstretched and still as the final notes faded.

She rose lithely to dispel the relaxed mood of the cool-down exercise. She frowned slightly. It occurred to her that too often this afternoon her thoughts had wandered away from the task at hand and materialized into an image of Beau Rutledge. It was disconcerting. She'd found her thoughts leaping uneasily to the party tomorrow night when she would surely run into him.

Not to mention Monday morning, the first day of their enforced . . . association.

She bent and caught up her towel in a brisk arc. She was too honest to deny that Rutledge's blatant interest in her as a woman didn't cause her a pang or two, but she was a professional, for heaven's sake! She would handle this assignment just as though Rutledge was any other Peabody client and she didn't have a scrap of intimate knowledge about his life and times in Atlanta. On that bracing thought, she mopped a dewy sheen from her face, looking forward to the sauna.

The trouble was that the man was just too sexy for his own good. Or for my own good, she amended ruefully. Why couldn't Ted Lipscomb or . . . or Spencer Foley have a little of that . . . whatever it was that Beau had that made him so appealing? She squinted her eyes thoughtfully, trying to imagine a sexy Spencer, but it was hopeless.

She sighed, knowing she was being unfair to Spencer. Maybe she was just tired. By anyone's standards, the day had been trying. After her unsettling encounter with Rutledge that morning, Sidney had spent an hour at Jill's Place thoroughly enjoying the release she found in aerobic dancing. Later, after grocery shopping, doing the laundry and a dozen other Saturday chores, Jill had called to say that her regular jazz instructor had called in sick. Cheerfully, Sidney had agreed to pinch-hit. Then, as she was getting ready to go back to Jill's Place, her phone had rung and, on hearing Spencer's voice, all she'd felt was irritation.

She'd settled back with a resigned sigh, locking the phone beneath her chin while pulling on her leotard. "How are you, Spencer?"

"Busy, very busy, love. I'm sorry I haven't called as I promised, but things are happening here and I'm putting in some long hours."

Sidney made a sympathetic noise and stuck one foot in a shoe. It had been a while since she'd heard from him and she hadn't missed him one bit.

"How's your job coming at the Peabody?" he asked while she juggled the receiver, trying to put on a sweatband. "You are still working at the bank, aren't you, Sidney? You haven't strayed into another unsuitable situation like that private detective thing, have you?"

Sidney stared stonily at the message board on the wall, feeling her nerves tighten. Nothing irritated her more than Spencer's anxiety that she might stray again from the straight and narrow. "I'm still at the Peabody, Spencer," she said evenly.

"Good," he said with the air of a father commending a wayward child. "And what about dinner tonight, love?"

Sidney had searched the ceiling for a reply. Why did he call her love? She didn't want Spencer calling her love. She'd never met the man she wanted to hear endearments from, she told herself, banishing an immediate image of a man smiling lazily into her eyes. Beau Rutledge, with his sun-streaked hair and tanned skin, had that determined glint in his gold eyes that gave him the look of a tawny pirate. He...

"Have you eaten there yet?"

"What?" Sidney jerked her thoughts and her senses into line. "I'm sorry, Spencer. I'm already dressed to go to Jill's Place. Maybe another time."

He was silent a moment. "Jill's Place. Oh, you mean the fitness center?"

"Right, Spencer. Jill Sinclair's place."

"Sidney, this is straight physical fitness stuff and not that belly dancing you taught in Las Vegas, isn't it?"

"Tahoe, Spencer," Sidney corrected patiently. "Not Las Vegas."

"Whatever," he returned dismissively. "I was just checking. I'm never certain about you. It worries me that you get these peculiar urges to do outrageous things, Sidney. I never understood why anyone with a degree in accounting would run off across the country to teach belly dancing. Or even more to the point, why would anyone ever *want* to belly dance?"

It was at that point that Sidney had lied and told him her doorbell was ringing....

"Okay, everyone, see you Monday!"

At the sound of Jill's voice, Sidney gladly pushed Spencer out of her mind. For a second, she debated whether to watch Jill's gymnastics class run through a routine or to go on to the sauna. A smile teased her mouth as she observed the antics of half a dozen teenage girls working out on the equipment at the far end of the room. All wore identical T-shirts with "Jill's Place" stenciled on the front.

"Megan, be careful on that crossbar!" Jill called. "Be sure your balance is under control before you attempt a maneuver like that."

Sidney singled out Megan's flaxen head easily. The girl's coloring was very similar to her uncle's, right down to the tawny eyes. When she'd first learned of the accident that took Megan's parents, Sidney hadn't connected Megan's name to the Rutledge case she'd handled in Atlanta. She'd been stunned to see Beau at the funeral. His attitude to his mother and Megan that day had been tender and loving, really remarkable considering everything Sidney knew about him.

Her mouth firmed. Anyone could manage respectable behavior for a limited time, she supposed. Even
Beau Rutledge.

Sidney reached down to untie her Adidas. It was hard
to reconcile the Rutledge she knew with the indulgent
uncle Megan raved about. The teenager never missed a
chance to tell Sidney about the wonderful Beau Rutledge—how kind and good-natured he was, what a great
sense of humor he had, not to mention his good looks.
Jill had been quoting Megan when she'd pronounced
Rutledge a hunk. It was obvious that Megan couldn't
understand why all the glowing reports of her uncle had
failed to ignite an answering spark in Sidney.

She turned casually, her expression amused as she
watched the slim pert sixteen-year-old. It was just as
well that Megan hadn't been at the bank today to see
Sidney's reaction to Rutledge. She would never let it
alone. Sidney was already regretting making that mischievous remark to Jill about his eyes.

As she studied Megan's confidence on the practice
mat, she was happy to see no trace of the apathy that
had fallen over Megan after the accident that had taken
her parents.

"Megan!"

Sidney froze, her eyes flying to the agitated girls just
in time to see Megan suddenly pitch forward, over-
shoot the practice mat and land hard on one foot and
an elbow. In a flash, Sidney and Jill were beside the
young girl.

Jill carefully felt the bones of Megan's ankle through
her bright magenta leotard. When the dazed girl
winced, Sidney anxiously scanned her pupils, looking
for signs of concussion. Thankfully there were none.
Apparently Megan had not cracked her head in the fall.

"Just lie still, honey," she soothed huskily.

"Let me know if this hurts," Jill said, probing an ankle lightly with her fingers, stopping instantly when Megan inhaled sharply.

"Boy, that was really stupid!" Megan muttered through white lips, shaking her tawny head in disgust.

"Anyone can have an accident," Jill sympathized, intently examining the already swelling ankle. She shifted slightly, allowing Sidney to take a look. Both were familiar with the injuries inevitable to dancers and gymnasts.

"My elbow hurts a little," Megan ventured with uncharacteristic meekness.

Jill transferred her attention to Megan's arm with professional briskness, then met Sidney's eyes with a knowing look. Sidney knew that Jill had caught a glimpse of Megan's trembling mouth. "I believe you've hit on a good excuse to get out of practice for a few days, Megan," Jill teased.

"Terrific," Megan muttered.

"I think it's going to need to be x-rayed, honey."

"I'll take her, Jill," Sidney offered. "You've got at least two more classes scheduled."

"Thanks, Sidney," the petite woman said with relief. "I don't know what I would have done today without you." She slipped one arm around Megan while Sidney supported the girl on the other side.

"It was nothing, I was glad to help out." Sidney smiled, accepting an ice pack from one of Megan's friends. If the truth was known, the hours she'd spent today at Jill's Place had been pure pleasure. Dancing relaxed her as nothing else could.

"Let's get this ice pack tucked into place," Jill murmured after they'd settled Megan into the rear seat of Sidney's Rabbit.

"Cheerleader tryouts are scheduled in two weeks!" Megan wailed, eyeing her swollen ankle with dismay. "This ankle better be okay by then." Anxiously, she sought Sidney's eyes. "Do you think it's hopeless, Sid?"

Sidney crossed her fingers mentally, but her expression was cheerful. "Most sprains are okay in two weeks as long as you stay off them. We'll do what the doctor says and you'll make those tryouts, for sure."

Megan looked doubtful but resigned, and Sidney's heart went out to her. The girl had certainly borne a lot of disappointment lately. She hoped this wouldn't be another one. In Sidney's opinion, Megan needed the satisfaction and involvement that came with being a cheerleader to compensate, in small part, for the loss of her parents.

"I'll notify your grandmother as soon as we arrive at the emergency room, Megan," she said, her eyes on the road. "I'd like to avoid upsetting her, but I don't see how we can. She has to know you've been hurt."

Unspoken between them was the tragedy Katherine Rutledge had already suffered. The elderly lady had looked so fragile at the funeral of Megan's parents.

Megan sighed, cupping her elbow in one palm. "Let's don't tell Grammy just yet, Sidney. I know where Beau is. The restaurant is on the way. You can run in and tell him what's happened while I wait in the car. My ankle is sore, but I don't think it's broken."

"Your uncle?" Sidney's voice was cautious, her eyes flicking uneasily to Megan's in the mirror, then back to the road.

"You know, the infamous Beau Rutledge," Megan chuckled, her good humor returning. "I guess you're going to meet him at last, Sid." Sidney heard the amusement in the girl's voice, but kept her eyes on the road. "We've got to have proof of insurance, haven't we?"

"I'd planned to talk them around that," Sidney muttered, not about to admit to Megan that she'd already met Rutledge. Twice in one day was one time too many. As it was, she'd been plagued all afternoon by recurring images of how his hand had reached to touch her hair. The deep husky pitch of his voice had lingered in spite of all her brisk efforts to banish it. How would it be to have him whispering soft words, sensual words...?

"He's having dinner at the Sugar Mill," Megan informed her helpfully, not bothering to disguise her delight that her two favorite people were to meet at last. "Just turn left at the next light. You can run in and tell him the gory details and he'll take it from there." Her tone was cheerfully confident. "He's a take-charge man."

Without a word, Sidney whipped the car into the restaurant's parking lot and stopped. She was in an illegal zone, but with Megan's ingenuity, she didn't doubt any protest would be dealt with.

"I'll be right back," she said evenly.

"No problem," Megan sang out.

If I hadn't seen Megan take that tumble, Sidney thought, *I'd wonder if I was being set up.* Even though she'd been ignoring Megan's unsubtle remarks about her uncle for weeks, the girl just wouldn't quit. Sidney groaned inwardly just imagining Megan's delight when she discovered that Beau and Sidney would be working together every day. Trying to keep up an attitude of indifference under the girl's shrewd eyes was going to be difficult, Sidney realized. And she was honest enough to admit that, up close, Rutledge was pretty devastating. All that virility and male appeal directed to a woman he fancied was formidable. He was a dangerous man and probably a dishonorable one on top of that. She would do well to remember it.

Grimly, Sidney entered the restaurant and waited for the maître d', feeling very conspicuous in her leotard and warm-up jacket. Her chilly expression quelled several warmly appreciative looks that reminded her of Rutledge when he'd cornered her on the stairs. After tonight, he was going to think she never put on ordinary clothes. She shifted restlessly. It was disgusting, this preoccupation with Megan's uncle. What did she care what Beau Rutledge thought?

"May I help you, madam?"

The maître d' was giving her a repressive look, taking care to avoid eyeing any part of her below her chin. Here at least was one man who wasn't impressed by her legs.

"I'm sorry," she apologized. "This is an emergency and I was told Mr. Rutledge is having dinner here. I must see him."

Pained acceptance settled on the man's smooth features. "Of course. Right this way, madam." He turned and started to walk away. Sidney was left debating whether to call out to him requesting that Mr. Rutledge come to her, or to simply follow the maître d' as though a woman dressed in a dance leotard in an exclusive restaurant was perfectly ordinary.

The maître d' stopped after a few steps, turned and gave her an expectant look. Taking a deep breath, she hurried after him, ignoring the blatant masculine approval that followed their progress through the restaurant.

They found Beau Rutledge at a choice table in a very secluded section of the Sugar Mill. Dim lighting fell on the beautiful features of his dining companion. Her black hair was perfectly coiffed, her makeup flawless. In a peacock-blue silk dress, she was stunning. And Rutledge was giving every indication of enjoying the utterly enticing picture she made. That is, until he caught sight of Sidney weaving through the tables behind the maître d'.

For an instant, Rutledge simply stared. Sidney caught the stunned expression on his face and her own embarrassment increased. And then he grinned. It was a boyish spontaneous grin that told her how genuinely pleased he was to see her. It took a moment for Sidney to discipline her reaction. Why, she wondered resentfully, did her senses insist on leaping wildly in response to his wonderful smile? Firmly, she reminded herself of what she knew about this man. Beau Rutledge wasn't what he seemed, and she'd do well to stop this idiotic tendency to waste time thinking about him.

With a discreet nod, the maître d' left them. Sidney waited as Rutledge lazily rose to his full height, one brow arched in amused inquiry.

"We're going to have to stop meeting like this, honey," he drawled wickedly. Doggedly, Sidney withstood the appreciative gleam in his eye as he glanced at the figure she cut in the cursed leotard.

"Mr. Rutledge, please," she protested, glancing quickly toward the other tables. Without waiting for an invitation, she slipped onto one of the unoccupied chairs at the table. "I'm here because of Megan."

"Megan?" Instantly, the amusement left his eyes. He sat down, his gaze hard and alert. He had incredibly sexy eyes, Sidney found herself thinking. Warm and wonderful.

"Is she hurt?" he demanded curtly. "Where is she? Has she had an accident?"

"Yes, she—"

His eyes closed weakly. "I knew it. She shouldn't have the car at night!" he groaned. "My mother talked me into it, even though I *knew*—"

"She hasn't been in a car wreck," Sidney interrupted hastily. "She's okay. I'm going to take her to the hospital emergency room to get an X ray. Megan herself suggested we stop here first and let you know."

"For God's sake, woman, what's the matter with her!" he demanded, catching one of her wrists.

Sidney tugged impotently to free herself. "She took a tumble on the practice mat. She hurt her ankle and her elbow when she fell." As soon as Sidney finished the sentence, Beau started to rise. She caught his upper arm with her free hand, wanting for some reason to reassure him. Green eyes locked with topaz. Both were oblivious to the curious stares of the other diners. Something charged the space between them, making Sidney suddenly aware of the power of the biceps beneath her fingers. Quickly, her hand fell away and Beau reluctantly dropped her wrist.

Half standing, he asked quietly, "Is anything broken?"

"I don't know," Sidney returned softly, her own concern for Megan giving her voice a husky tone. "I'm pretty sure not, but it seemed safest to let a doctor tell us for sure."

Beau nodded once, then stood decisively. "Okay, let's go."

"Beau!" Startled, Sidney and Beau turned to the woman, who, until then, had been silent. The woman's patience seemed exhausted. Her dark eyes glinted as she threw Beau an indignant look.

He shrugged apologetically, flashing her a smile that he probably used to charm birds out of trees and brunettes into his lap, Sidney decided cynically. "Ronnie, this is a hell of a situation, but my niece needs me, as you heard Miss..." He glanced at Sidney, one brow raised expectantly.

"Sidney James," she said crisply.

"Sidney James," he repeated huskily, as though committing her name to memory forever. Sidney faltered a moment under the lambent look in his eyes and then firmly stepped out of his dangerous force field. She turned toward his date. "Please pardon me for interrupting your meal, um..."

"Rhonda Spelling," Beau supplied quickly. "Ronnie, I'm going to get a taxi for you, babe. I know you'll understand that I have to see to Megan."

Babe! Sidney looked blindly over the heads of the Sugar Mill's customers, disdain tipping the corner of her mouth ever so slightly. If "Ronnie" understood, as Beau with typical male naiveté assumed, she certainly wasn't showing it. The look on her face was pure outrage.

Once outside, Sidney would have ducked quickly into her car and waited for Rutledge, but he kept a firm hold on her. To her amazement, "Ronnie's" ill humor faded after a boyish apology delivered with the famous Rutledge know-how, leaving nobody unhappy.

As they reached the car, Sidney bent to open the door closest to Megan. "Here's your uncle, honey," she said quietly, watching Megan's eyes turn eagerly to Beau. It wasn't hard to understand the girl's adoration. This man was definitely hero material, Sidney thought ruefully. That devastating smile and those topaz eyes were a dynamite combination.

"What have you done to yourself, Meggie?" Beau leaned around Sidney before she could step out of the way, enveloping her in the woodsy, musky-male scent of his after-shave. "Let me see, sweetheart."

Sidney was rigidly still as Megan propped her leg lengthwise on the back seat. She tried not to jump when Beau's arm...accidentally?...brushed her breasts as he reached toward his niece.

He lifted the ice pack and examined Megan's swollen ankle. "Let's look at that elbow," he murmured, gently running long sensitive fingers along Megan's arm, flashing the young girl a sympathetic look when she winced in pain.

"Okay, baby, let's get to the hospital," he decided, straightening. He caught Sidney by the arm and ushered her aside so that he could close the car door. "Could I have your keys, please?" he asked, extending a palm confidently.

"My keys?"

"You don't mind me driving your car, do you, Sidney?" he said, giving her name a special sound. He flashed a smile that would have melted the resistance of a woman made of sterner stuff than Sidney, and she found herself meekly handing them over. He courteously opened the passenger door for her, seating her as though she were injured too and walked around to take possession of her car and the situation.

Megan hadn't exaggerated when she'd described Rutledge as a take-charge man, Sidney reflected twenty minutes later while waiting for them both in the visitors' lounge of the hospital. She was still a little dazed at the ease with which he'd managed everything. He'd dismissed his date, then shanghaied Sidney's car and finally overruled the nurse who'd suggested that the doctor might be an hour getting around to seeing Megan. And each obstacle had been overcome without a cross word to anyone. He'd worked his magic with charm and smiles and plain old-fashioned sex appeal, Sidney decided firmly.

"Nothing's broken, thank God."

Sidney was so deep in her thoughts that Beau was already sprawled in the seat next to her before she even realized he was back. She turned, meeting his gaze with a little jolt. For a second, to her shame, Megan and her accident were almost forgotten, but she pulled herself together. "That's wonderful," she said. "Megan would have been miserable sitting around waiting for a fracture to heal, especially with cheerleader tryouts in two weeks."

He chuckled. It had a deep sound that settled somewhere in Sidney's middle, stirring a response that was already in danger of spiraling out of control. "You know her pretty well, I see," he observed. "Thankfully we've been spared a six-week convalescence."

Wryly, Sidney acknowledged the truth of that, but refused to let him know that she shared his amused view of the situation. She found his sense of humor almost as appealing as his gentle treatment of his niece. She didn't want to discover any other qualities to admire in Beau Rutledge, so she chose to misinterpret his remark. "I'm overwhelmed by your unselfish attitude," she said with cool sarcasm.

Beau laid one arm familiarly over the back of her chair, shifting slightly so that he could study her thoughtfully. "Judging by the chilly look in your eyes, I must be having a problem with my public image. And I could have sworn Megan was extolling my virtues to you with all the enthusiasm of a good press agent." His eyes danced mischievously. "Because I've sure been getting glowing reports about you, Sidney darling."

Sidney groaned inwardly, knowing he wasn't exaggerating. "As we both know, Megan is a child," she countered stiffly.

"Out of the mouths of babies..." he murmured softly.

This had to stop. "*Mr. Rutledge*, I need to—"

"Beau," he inserted quickly. "I know it's a silly name, but take my word for it, the short form is better than the whole thing," he said with feeling.

Diverted, she glanced into his eyes. "What is it short for?"

He looked pained. "Would you believe Beaufort? John Beaufort Rutledge."

She smiled. "Why not John if you hate Beau so much?"

He tilted his head, laughing at her through a tangle of incredibly long lashes for a man. "On second thought, it sounds just fine coming from you."

She felt the slow flush that crept upward, cursing her fair complexion and Rutledge. By the look on his face, he obviously enjoyed flustering her.

"Let's just say I don't believe my father approved of me quite enough to allow me the use of his first name."

Before she could explore that, he said with convincing sincerity, "Did I say how grateful I am that you rushed to Megan's aid tonight? And all teasing aside, I can see why she's been singing your praises for weeks now. She's got good taste."

Sidney stifled a quick rush of pleasure at his words. In spite of all the self-confidence she'd acquired in her twenty-five years, she discovered she was a tiny bit susceptible to the techniques he used to seduce his women. Uneasily, she resisted the thought. A woman was seduced only because she allowed herself to be. That couldn't possibly happen to her. She, of all people, knew what a womanizer Rutledge was. That knowledge was all she needed to resist him.

"You don't need to thank me for helping Megan," she said. "I was happy to do it. She's a sweetheart."

"Yes, she is." His eyes traced the curve of her lashes, her cheekbones, her mouth, before dropping to linger a second longer than necessary on the enticing fullness of her breasts in the skimpy top. By that look, Sidney knew he didn't think Megan was the only sweetheart, and it made her more aware than ever of her provocative outfit.

A little devil danced in his eye when she primly crossed her arms. "Don't you ever wear any clothes?" he teased.

She sighed, wondering if it were even possible to keep this man at a distance. "This is a perfectly respectable outfit for working out," she defended, hanging on to her composure by a thread. She'd never been subjected to such unqualified male approval at such close quarters! It was disconcerting, to say the least.

"Don't get me wrong," he said, settling more comfortably. "I'm not complaining." He crossed one long leg, resting an ankle on the opposite knee.

"Please don't do that," Sidney objected.

"Am I staring?" He laughed ruefully. "You're really something, Miss Sidney James, you know that?" Briefly, he allowed himself one appreciative assessment of her. "And I love your outfit almost as much as those pink shorts this morning."

Sidney forced herself to withstand the sensual assault of his eyes. After all, she wasn't Megan's age, although for two cents his faultless technique might threaten the logic and practicality she prided herself on. "I've been in and out of Jill's Place today. I only ran by the bank this morning on the spur of the moment," she explained distantly, deciding to acknowledge their earlier encounter before he could.

"Otherwise, you would have avoided me."

She glanced up, startled.

"Maybe I can change your mind," he said, looking like a big tawny tomcat.

Sidney made a small sound of protest.

"I'm going to work on it," he promised, his gaze intense on hers.

No, not a tomcat. A jungle cat.

He must have seen the tension on her face, because he seemed to relent suddenly. He leaned back against the side of the chair and eyed her with a little less hunger. "I asked Louis about you but you'd already gone and he couldn't tell me your name." He laughed softly, and Sidney braced herself against the deep appealing sound. "It wasn't any wonder you wanted to get away. I guess you could tell I wanted to grab you and carry you off."

What could you do with a man who had a tendency to inject an intimate note into every other sentence he said to you? Her expression cooled to discourage him.

"Fortunately," he announced confidently, "I can now tell that you are a very independent lady and the Neanderthal approach is all wrong for you."

She met his eyes squarely. "Every approach is going to be the wrong one coming from you, Mr. Rutledge."

He was still for a minute, assessing her thoughtfully, much as he had that morning. "Are you always so unapproachable, or is this something personal?"

She took a deep breath. "Do all the women you approach fall at your feet?"

He pursed his lips as though considering it seriously, but his eyes danced wickedly. "Without exception."

Her laugh was laced with exasperation. "You're impossible! Did anyone ever tell you that?"

"Nah, mostly they just fall at my feet."

"Are you ever serious?"

Grinning, he shrugged helplessly. "Only as a last resort."

Dangerous. Beau Rutledge was a dangerous man. She began to feel very sympathetic toward his ex-wife. And ex-secretary.

"You know," he said in a low husky voice, "it's too bad I didn't have enough sense to trust Megan's judgment. We could have been getting to know each other, sweet Sidney."

Not likely, she thought skeptically. Her eyes took on a speculative gleam as she imagined his reaction once he discovered how well she'd soon know him—or rather his business. The more she saw of him, the more she suspected he would not welcome her nosing around his territory.

One thing was certain—if he ever discovered her connection with the agency in Atlanta, she would find herself in a very delicate situation.

A little doubt surfaced as she scanned the hall, hoping Megan would appear. Her friendship with Megan complicated things. In fact, things were getting complicated all around. She didn't want to have anything to do with Rutledge but, at least until her job was done, she would have to deal with him business-wise. In the meantime, she was more than ever convinced that her first reaction had been the wisest—steer clear of Beau Rutledge.

"This is the first time I've actually looked forward to doing business with the Peabody," he informed her happily. "In fact, Louis roped me into attending some kind of command performance tomorrow night at the country club. Would you consider going with me?"

"Thank you, but I already have plans for tomorrow night," she said, not bothering to tell him the party was a command performance for her, too.

He looked disappointed. "Then how about dinner the next night?"

She was saved from having to reply when Megan appeared, awkwardly managing two shiny new crutches. "Megan!" she exclaimed, jumping up and rushing toward her. "Are you all right?"

Megan flashed a smile and swung an ankle wrapped in ace bandaging. "Ask me in ten days," she replied in cheerful resignation. "I've been promised I'll be okay by then."

"Don't worry, you'll make those tryouts," Sidney said confidently.

"You bet," Beau agreed. "Now let's get you home so you can get off that leg, honey." He turned to Sidney.

"I'll bring the car around if you'll wait at the entrance with Megan, Sidney." At her nod, he flashed his mega-watt smile and went to get the car. As soon as he was out of earshot, Megan turned eagerly.

"What'd I tell you, Sid? Isn't he a hunk? And sweet, too. How many uncles would drop everything to haul a pesky klutz to the hospital?"

Sidney drew a long-suffering sigh. "Any uncle with one iota of decency," she snapped. "Megan, I'm warning you, not one more word about Beau Rutledge or you *and* Rutledge can find other means of transportation."

Megan tipped her head and looked knowledgeably at Sidney. "Uh-huh," she said smugly. "Sparks are flying already. I knew this was a match made in heaven."

"Megan!"

Chapter Three

Beau Rutledge bent his head politely to catch whatever it was Clifton Rowe was saying. The chairman of the Peabody's loan committee was half a foot shorter than Beau and had a tendency to mumble. He was the sixth in a line of bank executives that Louis had trotted over for Beau to soft-soap. Immediately, Beau chided himself for the unfair thought. Why didn't he cut out this self-righteous garbage? Louis was going out of his way for him, so why didn't he just accept the favor? God knows, he needed all the help he could get. Why keep torturing himself because he wasn't in a position to resolve the difficulties at Rutledge by himself?

A troubled frown settled on his face. In his thoughts he quickly reviewed the incredibly swift reversal in the fortunes of the Rutledge clan. He was convinced there was more than just Ben's poor management at fault. His shoulders lifted in restless frustration. Time. He needed time to delve into the transactions of the past two years. He cursed his shortcomings. He was not an accountant, but he intended to familiarize himself with every facet of the company. His instincts told him something was wrong, and if he'd learned anything from Lisa and his ex-business partner, he'd learned to trust his instincts. Maybe he'd still have a marriage and the Atlanta operation if...

He smothered another curse and a surge of bitterness. *What was he doing!* His marriage and the fiasco of his business in Atlanta were in the past. He had put all that behind him. He didn't have time to waste by even thinking about it. He needed all his energy to cope with the immediate problem of keeping Rutledge Enterprises together.

He stared moodily at the bourbon left in his glass, wishing he could leave. Mr. Rowe was still dissecting the vagaries of the stock market. Beau struggled to resurrect his sense of humor. It could be worse. He hadn't sold his soul to the devil, he told himself—just mortgaged his birthright. He should be grateful Louis was sympathetic. Where else could he get a loan of this size?

But even as that thought formed, he rejected it fiercely. It was hardly a favor the Peabody offered. There was no risk for the bank. Rutledge collateral was lined up and it was highly desirable, he reminded himself grimly. He had chosen the only course of action available to him. The loan was crucial. It was as simple—and chilling—as that.

Longingly, he stared at the door, idly twirling all that was left of the Peabody's good bourbon. Fifteen more minutes, he promised himself, and then, good politics or not, he was leaving.

He tipped the bourbon to his mouth, his gaze roaming around the room, speculating about the posh crowd.

It was amazing how little the glitter mattered when his family's business, their lifeblood, was threatened. Impatience gripped him. His uncompromising nature demanded action. Now.

Vaguely, he heard Mr. Rowe curse the interest rate. Beau made sympathetic noises, wishing again that Sidney hadn't refused him when he'd asked her to come with him tonight.

Sidney. There was something about her that took his breath away. He stared down into his drink, seeing her face. She'd been so sweet to Megan last night, sincerely concerned. What a wonderful mother she'd make. What a wonderful lover she'd make! He couldn't remember ever being so quickly captivated by a woman before.

He was jostled from behind by an attractive woman, and when their eyes met, he apologized automatically, hardly noticing her. She moved away reluctantly and his eyes took on a troubled look. It didn't take much perception to see that for some reason Sidney was far from captivated by him. He hadn't missed her eagerness to get away from him or the hint of disapproval she'd leveled at him. And he couldn't understand it. She didn't even know him. Had she been influenced by the old stories of his rebellious days before he'd left Memphis? Had Megan, even unintentionally, somehow influenced Sidney against him? He moved his broad shoulders restlessly. He'd convince her otherwise if she'd only give him a chance.

Beau knew his strengths and he knew his weaknesses. When he wanted something, he went after it. He wanted Sidney and he planned to have her. She was warm, gentle—and very feminine. For some reason she was reluctant, but he'd work on building her trust in him. She was perfect for him. He'd already experienced the disillusionment that comes from incompatibility and he wouldn't make that mistake again. Lisa had been a supermotivated career woman with few morals. Their marriage had been doomed from the start. It had taken him a few months to see it, and by then it had been too late.

Sometimes he'd wondered whether Lisa had soured him forever. He let his imagination settle on Sidney, calling to mind the way she looked in her pink shorts, her russet hair all tousled and untidy. The thought triggered a rush of heat that spread through the length and breadth of him like warm honey. He hid a little smile. Sidney James was meant for him. All that remained was getting her to admit it.

Fatalistically, he gave himself up to fantasy, tuning Mr. Rowe and the stock market out. He pictured fiery hair spread across a pillow, his pillow. He imagined green eyes dreamy with desire—for him. He thought of her creamy skin, her delectable curves. It was enough to send his senses reeling. He tossed off the rest of his drink and was sending an impatient look over the well-dressed crowd when he saw her across the room.

Delight shot through him. She was beautiful in a black dress with her vibrant hair loosely fastened on the top of her head with an ivory comb. He allowed himself to feast his eyes on her, the sight of her sending his blood coursing through his veins.

Her dress was a high-necked affair, softly gathered at her throat. It had a demure look, he saw, deciding affectionately that it suited her. He smiled when she laughed at something someone was saying. As though tugged by an invisible cord, he simply walked away from Mr. Rowe, unaware of the man's startled look but irresistibly drawn to Sidney. He watched her reach forward and accept a drink. When she did, the black silk separated, baring her back from neck to waist. Beau's eyes flared hungrily. Not so demure, he thought ruefully, resisting an urge to pull her against his chest to protect his woman from other predatory eyes.

Sidney had known the moment Beau Rutledge walked into the room. She'd also made certain he'd not seen her. She refused to admit that she was actually hiding. Why should she? Hide, that is. She wasn't some kind of helpless rabbit, for heaven's sake. Now she closed her eyes, refusing to look at him, bringing her wineglass carefully to her lips. She sipped the crisp Chardonnay, but tasted nothing.

"Sidney, who *is* that gorgeous man?" said Elaine Whitman, the Peabody's head teller.

Sidney's vague reply was lost in the wild rush of her senses. But she made an effort to concentrate, staring into Elaine's face, refusing to succumb to the urge to turn and look at Beau.

Elaine said something else, but the words just floated around Sidney. It was the strangest thing. All her instincts were sharply alive, but not from the stimulation of the party, the people or the wine. It was Rutledge.

Who was the real Beau Rutledge? She'd like to know the answer to that one herself. Last night when they had delivered Megan to her grandmother, the thought uppermost in Sidney's mind had been getting away from him. She hadn't wanted to see him as a perceptive loving man. But only a fool could deny that was exactly what his attitude to his niece and his mother had been. So at odds with what she knew about him.

"Whoever he is, he's coming this way!"

Elaine sounded thrilled. Not Sidney. She had a quick mental image of him last night, walking her to her car, confidently assuring her he meant to drive her home and take a taxi from her place. She'd said no. And when he'd tried to wring from her a promise to see him again, she'd said no to that, too.

She might have been successful in avoiding Beau but there was no way she could avoid her thoughts. He had invaded the inner region of her mind in spite of her efforts to keep him out. Was the inevitability of their meeting tonight the reason she'd been especially careful when she'd dressed for this party?

Her gaze wandered to a full-length window where she could study her reflection. The black silk with its back slash and her flamboyant hair combined for a look of utter sophistication, and she felt a little surge of confidence. She took another sip of wine, then froze. Her senses prickled in warning.

If he'd been equipped with bells, she couldn't have been more aware of him.

"Hello, Sidney."

"Mr. Rutledge." Her gaze bounced off him. She inclined her head politely, hoping that her lashes screened the leaping response of her pulse.

"Back to that, are we?" he drawled, smiling with boyish charm at a gaping Elaine as he drew Sidney gently away. "Can't you bring yourself to call me Beau?"

"Not really," she said.

"Aw, come on."

She laughed in spite of herself, and for a moment he simply enjoyed the thrill of her smile.

Sidney tried to hide her face by turning her attention to her wine. Nervously, she gulped some and immediately collapsed in a fit of coughing.

"That's no way to treat good wine," he chided.

Choking, she nodded, her eyes beseeching when her breath didn't return. Quickly, he patted her once or twice between her shoulder blades, refusing to allow himself to stroke the silken skin that beguiled him in the backless dress. "You're taking an awful chance letting me revive you this way," he muttered, discreetly maneuvering her behind a large leafy schefflera when he saw that she was embarrassed.

"Why?" she sputtered, feeling foolish.

"Do you have anything on under this dress?"

She'd recovered her breath, but his remark nearly stole it away again. She found herself leaning weakly against him, nestled in the curve of his chest and arm. They fit together snugly, like puzzle pieces. Even when his warm hand glided from the middle of her back to her waist, she still didn't move. *Could she move?* He was tall and strong, all male. She caught the scent of the same after-shave and soap that had assailed her senses last night.

His gaze was fixed intently on her mouth. "Why didn't you tell me you would be here?" he asked quietly, his look taking in the cameo perfection of her skin.

Sidney pulled her scattered composure around her and stepped out of the haven of his arms, firmly stifling the quick disappointment that flared within her. *I will not be seduced by sheer animal attraction,* she told herself bracingly. "Why should I?" she replied coolly. "I told you I had plans for tonight. Beyond that, I didn't see that my plans were any of your business."

Playfully he threw out his hands and grimaced ruefully. "Uh-oh," he groaned. "I guess I'm coming on
too strong again. Tell you what, let's back up a few
paces. Even if it kills me, I'll exercise a little restraint.
We'll talk a little about. . ." He cocked his head as
though pondering what subject she'd enjoy. "Aerobic
dancing, fashion trends, cooking..."

"You see me as a little domestic?" she asked, one
brow arching.

"What's wrong?" He smiled, eyes warm. "Was I
way off?" He shifted his weight onto one leg and leaned
a shoulder against the wall.

Between the size of the schefflera and Rutledge's solid
frame, they were more or less isolated from the rest of
the crowd. She wasn't quite sure how he'd managed it,
but all of a sudden, she felt almost as though they were
alone, just the two of them. And the feeling left her too
vulnerable for comfort. What was this feeling of
breathless anticipation?

"Excuse me," she breathed. "The ladies' room—"
She fled, berating herself for her cowardice while
drawing a relieved sigh at getting away from him. She
found the powder room and ducked inside, staying in
one of the cubicles as long as possible without causing
undue curiosity from the attendant. She washed her
hands and, while drying them, finally forced herself to
glance in the mirror at her own reflection.

This is absolutely ridiculous, she silently lectured
herself, a determined glint in her green eyes. I'm twenty-
five years old. I've met men before who had everything
Rutledge has and I've never fallen into a state of total
confusion. True, he's got his share of charm, intelli-
gence, wit and looks, but since when does all that,
packaged in one man, do me in?

Since yesterday, a little voice whispered.

Sidney whipped around and headed for the door. She needed a little time to work out the mixed emotions that Rutledge evoked in her. The sensible, levelheaded Sidney knew him for a womanizer and worse, as far as his business dealings went. He was sweet to Megan and good to his mother, but so what? Otherwise, he was an unscrupulous person. Knowing that, she shouldn't respond to this urge she had to sample the delights promised in his warm and wonderful eyes. It was crazy! The same craziness had lured her off to St. Thomas, Nevada and Atlanta. It was just that it had never lured her into the arms of a rogue like Beau Rutledge! She grabbed the doorknob. One thing she knew for sure—she was not going to give him another chance to work his wiles on her tonight. She was going to find Louis and tell him she had a headache and go home. She'd done her duty by coming tonight, but enough was enough.

She stepped into the hall and glanced around. Seeing no one, she hesitated a moment, uncertain of the club's layout. When she'd dashed in here, she hadn't paid any attention to anything except escaping. Now she headed back in the direction she thought she'd come, taking a turn to the left and entering the first doorway on the right.

Inside she sighed impatiently, seeing that it was the club's administrative office. She turned to leave and bumped into something big and solid and warm.

"Don't run, Sidney."

Her eyes, wide and wary, flew to his. Lighting in the little office was dim, but she could still see stark desire flaring in his eyes. She didn't want him to know how trapped she felt, so she managed a wavering smile. "I took the wrong turn, I guess. I was just getting ready to leave."

"Can I take you home?"

"No!" Her hand was flung out defensively. "I mean, thanks, but I have my car. I can't just leave it here."

"Then you didn't come with anyone?"

She debated lying, but she'd had enough of her own ambivalence as far as this man was concerned. "No, I came alone."

He smiled. "And you intend to go home alone, right?"

"Right. Look, Mr. Rutledge, I don't know why you persist in playing this game."

"Why do you persist in trying to hold me off?" he countered.

"Will you stop it!" Her eyes flashed and she made a move to duck around him and escape through the door, but he moved easily to block her, closing the door deliberately.

"Can you honestly deny that you didn't feel something special a few moments ago when I held you in my arms?" he asked quietly.

Sidney stared at him, wishing she didn't know exactly what he was talking about. She wished she didn't think he looked wonderful in his charcoal suit and dazzling white shirt. She wished she didn't know what she knew about him.

"Didn't you melt against me? Weren't you aroused when we touched?" Before she could deny it, he added insistently, "Only for a second, I'll grant, but long enough to have a glimpse of what it could be like for us."

She told herself that, indeed, she would die before she admitted there was one word of truth in what he was saying. Nonetheless, this seemed to be one of those times when to say nothing was best. She averted her chin and tried to escape once more, her expression as cold and disapproving as she could make it.

Beau touched her cheek lightly. "You're not going to give us a chance, are you, Sidney?"

They exchanged a telling look. Self-disgust made Sidney sound harsh, and all her loathing was in her voice. "Not on your life, Mr. Rutledge. It takes more than a few suggestive words and steamy looks to seduce me. And now, I would appreciate it if you would let me pass."

The warmth that had softened the rugged angles of his features was gone. His mouth firmed as he studied her thoughtfully. "I guess you couldn't put it any plainer than that," he said dryly. "But just as a matter of passing interest, what is your problem? I can see that you don't like me. But why? You have to know someone to dislike them, don't you?"

More flustered than ever, she darted to the door, fumbling for the knob. "I can't believe this!" she muttered, jerking her hand back as she encountered not the door, but Rutledge's trim waist.

He looked at her in silence, then closed his hands on her arms. "What's the matter? Hasn't that cool reserve ever been threatened before, darling Sidney?"

"Stop calling me that!" she cried. "And turn me loose." How had she landed in this impossible predicament, she wondered wildly, looking around, knowing there was no one to witness this . . . this outrage.

The little office was deserted, cozy even. One lamp glowed softly, throwing an inviting circle of light on an assortment of magazines on a table before a couch. It was the perfect setting for a seduction scene.

Frantically she pushed that thought away. Not fifty feet down the hall, a hundred guests were eating and drinking. She was in no danger from this man even if his eyes did reveal desire.

"Believe this then, Sidney," Beau muttered, pulling her fully into his arms. And before she could escape it, his mouth came down on hers.

And, oh, it was good. She'd known it would be. This was what she'd feared from the first. This was why she'd fled to the ladies' room. His lips were warm and soft. There was nothing remotely brutal or aggressive about his kiss even though he'd been irritated and frustrated with her. It was sweet and imploring.

His touch on her arms gentled. One hand stroked up the curve of her shoulder, grazed the line of her throat and cupped the back of her head. His thumb found the contour of her jaw and positioned her mouth just so. She stood impassive as long as she could, but when his tongue sought entry with a sure thrust, she parted her lips helplessly.

Everything that was feminine in her blossomed in response to the taste and feel of him. She made a half-stifled moan and simply leaned into his embrace. Her hands lifted, settled on his shoulders, then compulsively slid into the gold-shot thickness of his hair.

His hands were at her waist, and then on her midriff, skimming along the soft outer curves of her breasts. One hand brushed at the black silk and plunged into the back slash of her dress. His palm was warm and questing on her skin. He groaned, and rested his mouth against the corner of her lips. "I knew it would be this way. I knew exactly how you would taste, how you would feel.... I knew how good we'd be together."

Released from the magic of his kiss, Sidney came back to earth with a thump. She opened her eyes, trying to bring her reeling senses in line. In some distant corner of her brain, she was aware that Beau was as disturbed as she by the impassioned kiss. Like two players who had forgotten their lines, they simply stared at each other. His chest was heaving as though he'd been running. The back of her hand was pressed against her mouth.

"I'll take you back," he said. He caught her hand and together they went into the hall. Sidney saw that the proper door to the ballroom was directly across from the little office. Dazed, she went toward it.

"Here you are!" Louis Maynard beamed at them both. "I see you've introduced yourselves. I lost sight of Beau a while ago, Sidney. I wanted to be sure the two of you got acquainted."

"Oh, we're getting acquainted all right, Louis," Beau said calmly. Sidney could feel his eyes on her but she refused to look at him. The devil!

"Fine, fine." Louis almost glowed with satisfaction. "I knew the two of you would take to each other. You know," he said directly to Beau, "I don't think we ever got around to talking about Sidney yesterday, what with one thing and another. But her credentials are top-notch. You can count on her being as professional an accountant as any CPA ever was. This lady—" his eyes rested on her proudly "—is almost uncanny when it comes to numbers, Beau. We've got this account that is a major headache every year. Well, last month she audited them and suggested a few changes. The end result was to simplify the whole thing. Has a natural gift, Sidney does. Yessiree, we're lucky to have her at the

Peabody, and you're lucky to have her at the plant for the duration of this loan."

"I thought she was your secretary." The hand at Sidney's waist flexed.

Louis laughed delightedly. "Don't I wish! But what a loss to accounting. Willy Sherwood would have my head." He looked at Sidney, still tickled. "Can you type, Sidney?"

"Enough to get by," she said evenly.

Louis's gaze went knowingly to Beau's hand, which was still firmly against the small of her back. "You know," he said expansively, noting their apparent unity, "I predict that once Sidney's at the plant, the two of you will find yourselves even more compatible."

"Will you excuse us, Louis." Beau's hand was compelling her now, urging her toward the large schefflera. Sidney thought about resisting, but it would attract attention—something she'd better avoid, considering the guests included everyone who mattered at the Peabody.

"Yes," he said through gritted teeth, uncannily reading her thoughts. "I would make a scene and you can't have that. You've got to think of your career." The last word was laced with a bitter irony.

He turned slightly so that his back was to the crowd and Sidney's back to the wall. She felt the same surge of vulnerability that had come over her earlier, only then he'd been teasing, indulgent. His eyes had flashed his appreciation of her as a woman he wanted. Now they glinted with...what? Gone was the mantle of charm and male interest. Instead, she read anger. Why was he angry?

"I guess you've been enjoying this little charade," he said silkily.

Comprehension dawned. He was irritated that she hadn't told him up front that she was assigned to Rutledge Enterprises. "You can think whatever you like," she retorted. "I wasn't under any obligation to tell you we'd soon be working together. You must know I didn't volunteer for this particular job."

He subjected her to a hard stare. "Your work is very important to you." Not a question, but a flat statement. Sidney had the ridiculous impression that she'd flunked an important test.

Her chin lifted proudly. "Well, of course. Isn't your work important to you?"

"Probably plan to be a Peabody VP in a few years," he speculated cynically.

"Mr. Rutledge, I don't think—"

He looked skeptical. "No?"

She controlled her own rising temper with difficulty. "What is this! Of course I hope to have a good future with the Peabody." Her look dared him to challenge such a sensible plan.

"Not much time for sticky relationships that might interfere with your upward mobility, hmm, Ms. James?" He gave her a searing, disdainful look. "I can see now that you're another one of those 'ladies with a plan.' No place in that plan for a man, babies, that sort of thing.... Tell me, does that plan keep you warm at night?"

Sidney stared stonily into his tawny eyes, wondering how she'd ever thought them warm and wonderful. But she'd been right about one thing. This wasn't a man who appreciated interference of any kind on his territory or in his personal life. Any wife of his had better be prepared to cater to a monumental ego. He certainly resented her more fiercely than she'd expected. *Arrogant, chauvinistic—*

He shook his head helplessly. "And you look so... You'll get a laugh out of this, but when I first saw you, you looked just like all my ideal fantasies packaged up in one beautiful image. Then last night you were so good with Megan." He made a short scornful sound. "But all of that is surface stuff, right? I'll bet the real Sidney is a shark at the old Peabody. Louis knew you could hold your own, that's why he's setting you up to hassle me."

She drew herself up to her full five feet five inches, torn between outrage and inexplicable hurt. Why was he so incensed at finding out who she was? Why did he speak of her job with such disgust? Was he that upset at being forced to tolerate a bank employee on his territory? Or did he have something to hide? Could it be something personal? She couldn't believe he'd have such an outdated attitude toward women in business. His wife had been a career woman, for heaven's sake!

She drew a long patient breath and looked him in the eyes. "Mr. Rutledge, I can't help what impression you got yesterday. If you'll recall, I did absolutely nothing to encourage you. In fact, I did everything I could do *dis*courage you."

There was nothing remotely amused in the slash of his mouth. "Well, I get the message now. I was a bit dazzled at first—and what man wouldn't be? But I've already made the mistake of falling for packaging, only to discover pretty shoddy contents inside. It's nothing personal, but I started thinking of you as a computer instead of a woman about five minutes ago."

Stung, Sidney's eyes flashed fire. "Well, believe me, I don't care *what* you think of me!" she blazed. "I'll tell you up front that I have no designs on you, mister. And your opinion of my femininity couldn't interest me less! If your local reputation alone hadn't been enough to put me off, then my own inv—"

She skidded to a halt, appalled at what she almost revealed.

He nodded curtly, backing slightly. "Then we understand each other."

"Without a doubt," she snapped, and whirled away in a swish of black silk.

Beau watched her leave, his tawny eyes unreadable. The soft sway of her hips might have beguiled him earlier, but now he quashed the same response ruthlessly. He went to the bar and ordered another bourbon. There was a certain appeal to her, he acknowledged with savage honesty. He recognized the feeling of hollow disappointment even though he despised himself for it.

She only looks like a darling, he told himself. Inside she was programmed for upward mobility, a career woman dedicated to her goals. From bitter experience, he knew anything else would come second—a distant second. There was nothing wrong with a woman having a career, but from Louis's glowing words and Sidney's own defense of her work, her job was everything to her. It probably took the place of a husband and children, friends, and he didn't want to get mixed up with another woman like that.

He tossed most of the bourbon off in one swallow. He didn't have time for a woman anyway. He set his glass down with a thump and left.

Chapter Four

Sidney had tried since 6:00 A.M. to deny the tingling sense of anticipation that hummed through her. It was the challenge of a new project, she told herself. She'd always been fascinated by the secrets that could be hidden in cleverly manipulated numbers. Certainly Rutledge Enterprises Inc. with its puzzling turnabout intrigued her. There were secrets galore there, and that was the reason for her unbridled eagerness.

In the shower, she found herself mentally reviewing her wardrobe. Already she'd rejected half a dozen perfectly adequate man-tailored suits. Why was it that her usual choices were suddenly unappealing, she wondered as she left the bathroom and went over to her closet.

After some indecision, Sidney finally settled on a peach silk blouse and a flared cream linen skirt. A multihued cummerbund that tied around her waist was the finishing touch. She surveyed herself critically. Was her appearance appropriate? Too feminine? She swung away from her mirror with a wry toss of her bright head. Okay, she admitted it. Without examining the reason, this morning she wanted to look...special. Beau's disparaging remark about her femininity had stung. She didn't dwell long on just why he'd managed to get to her, but he had challenged something basic and female in her.

No less than half a dozen times she'd told herself she didn't care a fig if he chose to believe her less of a woman simply because she was serious about her work. But still, that remark about her being a shark at the Peabody rankled in spite of her determination to consider the source. She didn't care what he thought about her. She didn't care whether he approved of her or not. Thinking of her as a computer instead of a woman, indeed! She glared into her breakfast yogurt.

She would be extra cautious in dealing with him, she told herself, rising and pouring the last of her coffee in the sink. And yet...the kiss they had shared was hard to forget. She thrust that thought away and grabbed her purse. Time to stop all this dawdling and do her job.

The complex that comprised Rutledge Enterprises was sprawled over six acres of land. The general offices had been built in the mid-fifties and adjoined a huge building materials retail outlet, one of three such outlets owned by Rutledge. As Sidney parked and headed for the front door, she recalled from the background workup that Louis had provided that there were three Rutledge-owned mills that processed the lumber from raw timber. All were located some distance west of Memphis.

For a minute Sidney felt sympathetic toward the man and the formidable job that he faced. It must have been traumatic for Rutledge to be forced to mortgage the land that supplied the raw materials for the mills. But as quickly as the thought came, she rejected it. Beau Rutledge was not a man who needed anyone's sympathy. Before the unsettling scene at the end of last night's party, he might have stirred a compassionate pang or two in Sidney, but no more. His amazing shift from would-be suitor to hostile businessman had been enough to convince her that he was a man who was well able to face down even formidable odds.

She discovered the reception area deserted, but she was a bit early. She glanced at her watch and walked to the window. She'd purposely planned a few minutes' respite before the inevitable encounter with Rutledge on his home turf, but now she wasn't so sure it would make a difference. If Rutledge's attitude last night was any indication, her job here wouldn't be easy, and a few minutes one way or the other wasn't going to help matters.

Idly, she adjusted the miniblinds to look out. The only thing moving was a tan and white Blazer rounding the blacktop drive in front of the office. She watched the driver deftly whip into the space closest to the entrance and stop on a dime. Sidney's pulse skittered wildly as Beau Rutledge emerged, his lean frame straightening with lazy grace.

Hastily she stepped back, plunging her hands into the deep pockets of her skirt. When he opened the door, she was facing him.

He stepped inside, his eyes flaring briefly at the sight of her before inclining his head in a perfunctory greeting. "Ms. James."

"Good morning," she murmured, her eyes taking in his casual white shirt and tan western-style pants. He looked like he'd be more at home outdoors than behind a desk, she thought, catching the smell of sunshine and fresh laundry and that woodsy male aftershave. His hair was rumpled, probably from riding with the window open in the Blazer and as she watched, he slanted restless fingers through it, pausing with a palm against the back of his neck in a tension-easing gesture.

"You're early," he observed, flicking a remote glance over her carefully chosen outfit. Gone was the teasing man with the lazy smile who'd pursued her so relentlessly. In his place was a hard-eyed businessman whose manner said plainly that he couldn't be less interested in her as a woman. After a two second assessment, there was not a hint of welcome in his tawny eyes.

Sidney's sense of humor bubbled up momentarily, mildly exasperated by the cool reception. He hadn't exactly been bowled over at the sight of her.

Suddenly she was shocked at herself. *What in heaven's name was she doing!* It was that crazy capricious streak again. She groaned inwardly. Was she to be plagued forever by these unbidden urges to do something foolish? Like lusting after Beau Rutledge? Faced with all six feet three inches of the man before her, she simply couldn't delude herself any longer. She was attracted to him, she realized with dismay. Fortunately, she'd recognized the symptoms before dashing headlong into something that she might have trouble getting out of.

Blast him, she fumed, looking away from eyes the color of scorched honey. What kind of man had eyes that color anyway?

She clamped her teeth stubbornly. It was going to take more than physical perfection and mesmerizing masculinity to make her abandon her professionalism! Wryly, she thought it ought not to be too difficult. It was obvious that he'd dismissed any personal interest he might have felt for her. That shouldn't surprise her. One thing she knew firsthand—his feelings were anything but constant. If he hadn't respected his marriage vows, he certainly wouldn't waste any time on a casual flirtation, especially now that he knew her to be the despised accountant from the bank.

She gathered up her briefcase and handbag. The message last night had been loud and clear—he tolerated having her only because he had absolutely no choice. With a mental squaring of her shoulders and a sigh faintly tinged with an emotion she refused to examine, she vowed to settle for the man's respect. And to regret nothing.

"Eager to get started, hmm?" he gibed, moving across the reception area toward a door that Sidney assumed led to the inner workings of his company.

"I was a bit early," she acknowledged. "And, yes, I am eager to begin. I need a couple of days just to get the feel of your computer system and the accounting procedures. Then I can—"

He stopped her with a hard look. "Just a minute, lady. You're not here to take over. I'll decide which areas of the company you'll have access to. Be assured that they'll be as limited as I can make them and still give Louis the numbers he needs."

Redhead or not, Sidney prided herself on controlling her temper, though she couldn't remember when it had been so difficult. Green eyes blazed into amber. Antagonism crackled between them as tangible as the hum of the air-conditioning unit. Fortunately, the outside door opened just then and a couple of startled employees entered, causing Sidney to bite off a sharp retort.

Beau made a frustrated sound, muttering something about "my office," and spun away from her. Sidney, counting to a slow ten, mastered an impulse to kick his arrogant . . . shins. Stomping after him, she indulged herself by hurling a few choice epithets under her breath at his broad back, knowing even before she opened her mouth that Rutledge was someone who would counter hostility from her with more of the same. Besides, that wouldn't earn his respect. And she was determined to carry out this assignment like a professional. Nothing would give him greater pleasure than to send her slinking back to the Peabody in defeat.

They turned a corner and he opened a door, pausing to allow her to step inside first. She stalked into his office and watched as he closed the door and shouldered his way around her. In several long strides he was beside his desk. He didn't sit down, but with a curt gesture indicated that Sidney should.

She debated for a moment, judging that in a sparring match she would retain some advantage by standing. But on second thought, she decided against it and sat down.

Professionalism, she cautioned herself grimly.

Beau deliberately propped one hip against his desk and, without looking at her, leaned over and punched an intercom. "Hold my calls, Gail," he ordered in an even tone. Then he turned back to Sidney.

"Let's get something straight right up front, Ms. James. You're barely inside the door and already you've outlined how you plan to work without consulting anyone. I have no doubt that without constraints, in a week you'd know everything there is to know about Rutledge Enterprises, right down to how I like my coffee.''

Sidney remained silent, her outrage building as Beau continued inflexibly. ''You, Ms. James, have everything to gain and nothing to lose by such a course. In fact, there would probably be a commendation in it for you,'' he surmised with undisguised contempt. ''Maybe even another rung up the corporate ladder.''

While she gritted her teeth, he went on. ''On the other hand, the Peabody doesn't own me or my company. They have just loaned me money. I agreed to allow them to monitor it, but I didn't agree that you, as their representative, could have unlimited access to Rutledge Enterprises.''

Never had Sidney wanted so passionately to speak her mind. This . . . this bully was deliberately trying to sabotage her! And his bad attitude wasn't a result of a business decision—it was strictly personal and directed at her. He'd been relatively resigned to the fact that an accountant was going to be on the premises of his precious company for the duration of the loan. Why was he so furious about it now? Wasn't it because the accountant turned out to be her?

''No comment, Ms. James?'' he taunted silkily, tapping a gold pen against a well-formed thigh.

''What would be the point?'' she snapped. ''If I say I have no intention of unearthing your company's deepest secrets, you won't believe me. If I deny that I want access to material unrelated to the loan, you won't believe that, either. You've outlined the ground rules. What's left for me to say?''

Something like wary respect flashed in his eyes, then was quickly gone. He straightened up and they stared at each other, their expressions grim.

"You'll be disappointed to find out that there are more ground rules, as you call them, than that." He stepped behind his desk and flipped open a folder. "I came in early this morning and worked up this list. On it are the names of the people you may contact to compile your reports to the bank. Gail Colson is my assistant," he said, explaining one of the few names on the list. "Oliver Petrie is head of administration. You do not have unlimited access to the computer or to the records in accounting."

Sidney drew in a deep, slightly shaky breath. "Mr. Rutledge, I understand your reluctance to have an outsider foisted on you, worse yet, an outsider who will soon have access to all your financial secrets—"

At that he shot her a look calculated to shrivel her up right where she sat. Sidney could feel the conflict seething in him. "Haven't I just explained that you *won't* be privy to any confidential material?" he said dangerously. "Look, lady, I borrowed money. I've already submitted a proposal showing exactly where that money is going. That's the extent of your intrusion into my company. I can't make it any plainer than that. I've already told Louis I won't have you second-guessing my decisions!"

"And how will the bank know for certain that you aren't using the money for something that you consider more important or more urgent than your original plan if they don't have full access to your records?" Sidney demanded with cool logic. "When you entered into the agreement with the bank, you gave the bank the right of access, Mr. Rutledge."

Grimly, Beau eased into his chair. His eyes were hard as the topaz they resembled. "You're enjoying this, aren't you?" he gritted.

Sidney fought down another moment of compassion for him. *The man doesn't need your tenderness,* she told herself, resisting a quick mental image of him comforting Megan with gentle hands and gruff-soft voice. And why was she suddenly hearing the deep quiet sound of his laugh when she had choked on the wine?

"I don't suppose you would believe me if I told you that I might be able to help you," she said quietly. "If you would just allow me to—"

He surged up, angrily slashing a hand in midair. "I'm not allowing you an inch, lady! I don't want any help from you, and I'm certainly not going to help you, either!"

She frowned. "What does that mean?"

"Don't expect any special treatment from my staff, Ms. James. If this job earns anything for you, it will be without anybody at Rutledge aiding and abetting you. So don't ask."

As if I would on threat of death! Sidney seethed inwardly. It was getting harder and harder to keep from hitting this guy! And to think I was starting to feel a twinge of sympathy for him. Hah!

Ignoring the angry frustration in Sidney's green eyes, Beau went on with bland arrogance, "First, I want copies of all your reports routed through me before you send them to Louis Maynard." He glanced up from the notes in the file.

"Fine," she snapped.

He nodded, a quick satisfied movement, before consulting his notes again. "If you speak with other members of my staff, expect them to report the details to me.''

''Mr. Rutledge,'' she said with exaggerated patience, ''don't you think you're being just a little bit ridiculous? I'm not your enemy, for heaven's sake! I'm on your side, whether you believe it or not. These silly constraints will only complicate my job and might prevent me from uncovering some problem that you'd benefit from knowing about.'' She leaned forward, her pose unconsciously alluring.

''Humor me,'' Beau growled, turning away from the sight of her cameo skin and soft enticing mouth, determined to resist her appeal. Stonily, he blocked out the scent of her perfume, something flowery and fresh. He argued with the perverse part of himself that wanted her, no matter what. She was eloquent and logical in defense of her work, but he wasn't getting mixed up with her.

''Is this decision final?'' she inquired calmly.

''You got it.''

''Well,'' she said briskly, ''show me where I'm going to be quarantined and I'll get on with it.''

Beau reluctantly admired her grace as she stood, her smile only slightly off. He crushed the suspicion that she was a little hurt by his attitude. She was going to be a troublesome opponent. It was better to think of her as an adversary, he told himself, or he might find himself tempted in spite of everything he knew about her. Hadn't she proved how totally she was committed to her work? His motions were swift and decisive as he closed the file with a snap.

''There's a small room a couple of doors down that has been unoccupied for a while,'' he informed her. ''You can have that.'' Even as he said it, Beau wondered at himself. She would be close. Too close. There were at least half a dozen places she could use for an office where he wouldn't see her except when she brought her reports for his review. Disgusted, he swung away from his desk. *Keep it up, Rutledge. For a man looking to avoid trouble, you're making some idiotic moves.*

Sighing, Sidney fell into step beside Beau. She felt as though she'd come through a grueling competition, but she certainly didn't feel victorious. This man was definitely going to complicate her life. Even after the negative reactions they provoked in each other, she was keenly aware of him: the breadth of his shoulder almost touching hers, the power in his stride as she skipped a little to keep up with him.

"You can leave your things here," Beau suggested, opening a door to a small, comfortably outfitted office. Sidney frowned, a little uncertain of her bearings. If she wasn't mistaken, this office almost connected with Rutledge's. She smothered a short rueful sound. She was going to be working practically within sight of him, for Pete's sake! The better to keep an eagle eye on her, she supposed, to prevent any infraction of his ground rules. With a little shake of her head, she gave up trying to figure him out. This job was definitely going to tax her professionalism.

"Gail will show you around," he said. "You can ask her for anything else you might need."

Sidney nodded politely, dropping her purse into a drawer. She set her briefcase on the top of the desk and looked around. All she really needed was space for her computer and calculator, plus a drawer or two for some files.

"Gail!"

At the abrupt summons, a tall pencil-thin brunette appeared through the door at Sidney's left. Her dark hair was cut in a boyish bob and her gray eyes were friendly. She smiled at Sidney with a hint of curiosity and Sidney warmed to her instantly, relaxing a bit. It was comforting to be on the receiving end of anything resembling human kindness, she decided. She could hold her own in most difficult situations, but she had just discovered that Beau Rutledge's brand of rejection was strangely unsettling. She refused to think she could be hurt by him.

"I thought you were going to be a man!" Gail Colson exclaimed, subjecting Sidney to an approving once-over. She turned to Beau with a teasing grin. "This is hardly the bald-headed myopic bachelor that you described Friday, Beau."

"Sorry to disappoint you," Sidney responded with a smile, accepting Gail's outstretched hand with another sidelong look at Beau. Why, he was embarrassed!

"I think I may survive," Gail quipped dryly, darting another quick look between her boss and Sidney.

Shrewd woman, Sidney surmised, liking her instantly. And unless she was mistaken, Gail sensed the tension that thrummed between Beau and Sidney even if she hadn't hit on any reason for it.

"I've been beating the bushes looking for office space for you," she informed Sidney. "And I've found two possibles. You can choose the best one."

Beau cleared his throat. "I've already taken care of it, Gail," he said quickly. "Ms. James can use Cheryl's office."

Gail looked even more interested. "You bet," she murmured, nodding slowly. "Cheryl is on a six-month maternity leave. Her office is perfect." She shot a look at her boss. "Why didn't I think of it myself?"

"Well, that's settled," Beau announced briskly, avoiding his assistant's eye. "Take care of her, Gail—ladies' room, coffeepot, that kind of thing." He shot Sidney a hard look. "I've briefed her on everything else that concerns her."

In the little silence that stretched as he left, Gail's look was speculative, darting between the unreadable expression on Sidney's face and her boss's figure as he left the room. "For a minute there," she said, "I was reminded of his daddy."

Sidney looked blank. "His daddy?"

Gail smiled. "Can I get you a cup of coffee?" At Sidney's vague nod, the woman went to the back of her office through another door to a small kitchen. Sidney followed slowly, more interested than she'd like to admit to hear about Beau's father.

"John Rutledge was an arrogant rigid man, and the company was his life," Gail said frankly, filling two cups. "Although I've only been working for Beau for three months, I can see a lot of traits they had in common."

"Uh-hmm, that's Rutledge all right—arrogant and rigid," Sidney muttered into her coffee.

Gail laughed. "Not those traits." She threw Sidney a quick look. "May I call you Sidney, or do you prefer Ms. James?"

"Please...it's Sidney. Only Rutledge calls me Ms. James."

Gail hid a smile behind her coffee cup. "Possibly because you call him Rutledge."

"What traits were you thinking of?"

Gail arched one dark brow, but went on obligingly. "Integrity, loyalty, a keen sense of fair play and sheer guts, if you'll excuse a four-letter word," she responded without hesitation. "You know the financial situation Beau faces, but you might not be aware of the conditions that existed when he took over just ninety days ago. His brother, Ben, was not the manager that John Rutledge was, or that Beau is. But everyone knew Ben was the old man's favorite. Still, Ben lacked a certain flair, and I suspect it had something to do with the fact that his father never allowed him to make mistakes or to benefit from the consequences of wrong decisions. He was never allowed to even make decisions," Gail explained. "Beau, on the other hand, left home right after college, having worked for his father in the company for barely a year."

"A personality conflict?" Sidney guessed.

"Right. Two strong-willed individuals with conflicting ideas. They butted heads daily. It couldn't work. Beau... Well, let's just say he had flair, the right stuff. But he and his father didn't hit it off and Beau left. He went to work for an international engineering firm based in Atlanta. He married a woman who was also an engineer, and they eventually went into business together with another man who worked with them. The firm was extremely successful," Gail said. Then, as though realizing she was revealing a lot of personal information about her boss, she added, "Everybody knows about Beau's stormy relationship with John Rutledge. And it's certainly no secret that he was very successful on his own in Atlanta." Gail's laugh was rueful. "Now if Beau can just do the same with the mess he inherited from Ben, everything will be fine."

Sidney sipped her coffee, marveling over Rutledge's amazing capacity for winning friends. She supposed she shouldn't be surprised to find that Gail Colson was another adoring fan since she was the man's assistant. But such a glowing testimonial!

Sidney slanted a speculative look over Gail's attractive face and sleek figure. It wouldn't be the first time Beau Rutledge had charmed a member of his personal staff. She flicked a glance to Gail's left hand, curled around the coffee cup. No ring. A swift sharp reaction that couldn't be jealousy was quickly subdued. She didn't want to believe there was anything going on between Gail and Beau. But even if there was, she decided briskly, finishing her coffee and bringing her thoughts into line, it was no business of hers.

". . . and so you just let me know."

Sidney's gaze went to Gail blankly, realizing that she had not heard one word in the past few moments. "I'm sorry, Gail, I'm afraid I didn't catch . . ."

"No problem, I was just saying that you'll want to meet Oliver Petrie right away. Accounting and data processing as well as payroll, shipping and receiving fall under Oliver's jurisdiction," she explained helpfully. "I'll give you a copy of the organizational structure of the company and you shouldn't have any difficulty."

Thoughtfully, Sidney went to the tiny sink and rinsed out her cup. Apparently Rutledge hadn't informed his assistant about the restrictions he'd taken such satisfaction in telling Sidney about. The material Gail mentioned would be very helpful. It would provide a more complete picture of Rutledge Enterprises.

The more informed Sidney was, the more efficient she could be. Sidney planned to be an asset to Beau whether he liked it or not. Another factor was that she needed

as much information as possible to follow up on Louis
Maynard's suspicions. She wasn't here only to track the
loan, and whether Rutledge agreed or not, the stub-
born mule was going to benefit from Sidney's "intrusion" into his company. A grim little smile touched her
mouth as she recalled his reaction when she'd told him
she was here to help him. She set her cup down with a
determined snap. The best thing would be to have as
little contact with him as she could manage.

Chapter Five

She managed it just fine, Sidney discovered with some chagrin, juggling numbers at her desk a week later. Avoiding Rutledge was incredibly easy since he seemed equally determined to avoid her. Or at least, he seemed to avoid any personal contact with her.

But she was always aware of him. Their gazes linked at unexpected times, his amber-dark and unreadable, hers green and equally guarded. The whole situation threw Sidney into a confused frame of mind that was as exasperating as it was unsettling. Yet she could read nothing in Beau's cool gaze, and thankfully it seemed that no one else was aware of their mutual antipathy. Apparently he intended to keep their differences private.

The only thing was, she found herself piqued by his cool detachment. And disgusted with herself for even noticing it. Was this some kind of game he was playing?

Her fingers raced over the keys of her calculator, dismissing such a ridiculous possibility. She told herself she was relieved that his initial interest in her had passed. Her fingers punched the wrong key and she impatiently cleared the error. She had no interest in Rutledge or his games. She was here in an official capacity. All she had to do was concentrate on that fact and ignore anything else. She knew the danger of getting mixed up with a man like that, didn't she? She reminded herself of his cavalier treatment of his wife and his obvious lack of remorse over it. She frowned at the thought, her pace on the calculator faltering along with the resentment that was becoming more difficult to sustain. It was hard to remember Beau's faults in the atmosphere of admiration that surrounded him at Rutledge Enterprises. It hadn't taken long to discover that practically everyone shared Gail Colson's opinion of Beau.

And, as much as Sidney hated to admit it, he deserved their admiration. He was a born manager. If the tidbits she'd picked up here and there were anything to judge by, he had indeed inherited a flair for business. He was a third-generation Rutledge, and in Memphis, the Rutledge name was synonymous with success. In fact, the more she observed Beau, the more it puzzled Sidney that his business in Atlanta had failed. She could have sworn the shrewd decisive qualities he exhibited daily were second nature. She couldn't imagine him operating his own interests with less expertise than he used here. It just didn't make sense.

The whole situation intrigued Sidney. It was just the type of enigma that she delighted in solving. But in the meantime, she sighed with faint regret, that particular mystery would have to wait. Today the first report to the bank was due.

She looked it over briefly, debating whether to release it immediately or give Beau time to read over his copy and then send it to the bank. She pursed her lips thoughtfully, wondering how he would interpret the last paragraph. She didn't have long to wait.

"Ms. James!"

She jumped at the sound, forcing down the instant leap of her pulse that seemed to be her standard reaction to Beau Rutledge. Unconsciously, she squared her shoulders and smoothed a quick hand over the russet cloud of her hair, tucking unruly tendrils away from her cheeks before turning her eyes to the door.

He came striding in with an air of dominance, his gaze as hard as flint and just about as hostile. Slapping some papers on her desk, he snapped, "I want this report changed!"

She slowly got up, meeting his eyes coolly. "I hope this isn't going to happen every week when you read my report, Mr. Rutledge," she remarked, adding silkily, "Was it anything in particular that made you unhappy?"

"Unhappy!" he barked, picking up the report and flapping it angrily in her face. "That's rich, that's really rich!"

"I agreed to give you a copy of my report, Mr. Rutledge, not allow you to dictate what it contains."

He glared at her, then flung himself into a chair. She watched him take a deep breath, almost reading his thoughts as he wrestled with his temper. She'd already observed his skillful handling of people and right now she suspected he was calculating the best tactic to use to outmaneuver her.

"Look, Ms. James, yelling at each other isn't going to accomplish—"

"You're yelling, Mr. Rutledge, not me."

"—accomplish anything," he said through clenched teeth. "You're supposed to track the loan, not conjecture on the future of Rutledge Enterprises!"

Her gaze surveyed the handsome man. With his tie loosened and the sleeves of his white shirt rolled up and baring tanned forearms, he looked rumpled, harassed and—she admitted it—very attractive. She sighed resignedly, trying not to be influenced by his appealing masculinity. "I assume you're referring to the last paragraph."

"You know I am, lady! What do you mean telling the bank that I'm on the verge of—"

"I didn't tell them any such thing!" she argued firmly. "And don't call me lady, if you please. I'm Ms. James, and I'll thank you to remember it."

For a moment, she thought he would explode with frustration, and before he could, she went on patiently. "For the benefit of anyone who might not want to plow through the numbers, that paragraph is simply a word picture of the figures in the report. It serves as a quick overall recap of the week."

"It implies I'm in trouble."

She sighed again, this time with impatience. "You are in trouble, Mr. Rutledge. You can't deny it."

He stood up and paced in front of her desk. "Did you have to point it out to them?" he demanded with grim frustration.

She looked at him wordlessly, berating herself for feeling concerned about him and his company. Her tenacious efforts at the computer had revealed some information that had alarmed her, but now she fought the traitorous compassion that he could arouse in her. What was it about him that triggered such emotion in her? She should be outraged that he was so quick to fault her, that he didn't hesitate to show her how contemptuous he felt toward her.

So why did she feel like going to him and smoothing back his rumpled hair, telling him that she believed in him, that he would pull it all out successfully in spite of the obstacles?

"Everything is black and white to an accountant, isn't it?" Beau said bitterly. "Dot every *i* and cross every *t*. Don't leave me any room to maneuver here. I might want to juggle ten or fifteen bucks around." He flicked a resentful look over her, making a disgusted sound in his throat. "Deliver me from a woman hell-bent on success."

Sidney's sympathy evaporated as quickly as rain in the desert, but he was gone before her sputtering outrage was vented.

Sidney put the incident over the report behind her and plunged into the job with renewed determination for the next two weeks. She knew Beau's reaction stemmed from the killing pressure of trying to keep Rutledge Enterprises alive. She had no desire to add to his troubles, but she had to do her job. Besides, whether he'd admit it or not, her meticulous tracking was an asset. Yet, she could see very little change in his attitude toward her and was disgusted with herself for even noticing.

She reached for a printout that she'd run only minutes before and frowned, rubbing a forefinger between her eyebrows thoughtfully. After careful tracking, there was a slight but unmistakable improvement in output, she noted, surprised at the satisfaction the discovery brought. One silken brow lifted wryly. *Anyone would think I had a personal stake in the outcome of all this.*

She glanced idly at her watch, then rose, tossing her pencil aside. She'd been working hard for an hour and it was only seven in the morning. Even for Sidney this dedication was hardly routine professionalism. For some reason, she felt a sense of urgency on this job. Something wasn't quite right, but she couldn't put a finger on it. It was possible that she was influenced by her suspicions about Beau's Atlanta operation. She still regretted having to drop that investigation before she'd uncovered exactly what was wrong. She was finding disturbing similarities—questionable entries, puzzling deletions.

Added to that, she was having difficulty getting information from Oliver Petrie. Ordinarily, she would simply bypass him and find her own sources among more cooperative employees, but Beau's restriction nixed that option. She wasn't to forge ahead on her own. Any material from data processing or accounting had to be processed through Petrie, who had been polite, but distinctly uncooperative. It was frustrating, to say the least.

Wearily, Sidney pinched the bridge of her nose with thumb and forefinger. Did Petrie have any vested interest in the stock options owned by Vince Trehern? From bank paperwork, Sidney had uncovered Trehern's options, which, apparently, had been one of the unfortunate legacies of Ben Rutledge's year of management. Trehern could exercise his options with a relatively small imbalance of profit, another fact that made Sidney uneasy.

Sidney had already resolved to talk to Beau about the threat posed by Trehern's options. She was just waiting for an opportune moment, she told herself. She refused to admit that she hoped Beau's attitude toward her would mellow and that he would come to her first. Obviously he was as suspicious as ever, otherwise she felt he would have dropped those silly constraints.

Sidney rubbed the small of her back and shrugged philosophically. It would take a little longer, but she was confident that she could eventually pull everything she needed out of the computer with or without Beau or Petrie.

She stretched her arms about her head and strolled to the kitchen, hoping to find something besides Gail's health food now that she'd worked up an appetite for breakfast.

No such luck. Her lips tilted in a small smile. As she'd feared, the refrigerator yielded yogurt, cheeses and salad makings. The cabinets were no better—raisins, banana chips, sunflower seeds and herb teas. She wrinkled her nose.

"Good thing I'm not picky," she muttered, munching on a handful of something natural-looking. She stooped to poke around in the refrigerator in search of something else—anything else—and found some croissants in a plastic box.

"My kingdom for sausage and a biscuit," she grumbled, settling for cream cheese. She spread it generously on the croissant and popped it in the microwave before reaching for the coffee decanter, only to remember that she'd forgotten to make coffee when she'd come in. Quickly, she filled the decanter at the sink. After a couple of minutes, the coffee started to brew.

She turned, looking for a cup and collided with Beau's broad solid chest.

"Oh! Excuse—"

"Sorry!"

They both spoke at once, then hastily stepped aside, but in the same direction. Sidney's nose almost touched the tawny thatch of hair that was visible in the open collar of his shirt. Her eyes flew to his, but something—a fierce flaring in the topaz depths—sent her gaze skittering off. She took in the familiar scent of him, fresh shirt, sunshine, outdoors. It caught at her breath, scattering her thoughts like confetti in the wind.

"Why are you here at this hour?" he growled, his eyes skimming across her face. She was quivering with tension and the wild crazy reaction that always set in whenever she was close to Beau. What a laugh he'd have if he ever found out what a single look from his incredible eyes did to her stupid heart. The thought jerked her limbs into life again, and she moved to the left just as he did the same.

Again their eyes met, and they both shifted a little warily. Sidney's heart thumped crazily in her chest, making it practically impossible to appear nonchalant. She was aware of him with every nerve in her body. He'd already discarded his jacket and his shirt was open, his tie loose. Not that it mattered. He looked good in everything from a three-piece suit to faded jeans, and it galled her that she even noticed. Heat spread through her when she saw his gaze fall on the thrust of her breasts in her soft pink blouse. Helplessly, she felt the tips quicken in response to the unmistakable male assessment.

"I never needed a traffic light in the kitchen before," Beau drawled, not moving away as quickly as he should have. Instead, he treated himself to a moment of just being close to her, breathing in that flowerlike scent she used, allowing his gaze to skim over her face. He frowned on seeing the smudges of fatigue under her eyes but stubbornly resisted an impulse to run a fingertip across the delicate skin. More than once lately, to his intense disgust, he'd caught himself reacting with the instincts of a protective male. What was it to him if she wanted to work around the clock? Weren't most of these career-crazy females like that?

"Aren't you slightly overdoing the dedicated career bit?" he said curtly, catching her at the waist and setting her aside. But his hands lingered on the alluring shape under his palms a second longer than was strictly necessary. Her scent was all around him, tantalizing and provocative. The first button on her blouse had come undone and he caught a glimpse of ivory skin, beguilingly dusted with a few freckles, before he tore his gaze away in a blind search for a cup.

"Did you want coffee?" Sidney asked in her husky voice, and he willed himself to withstand the bewitching sound. The woman had the sexiest voice he'd ever heard!

"How is Megan's ankle? I've been missing her at Jill's Place."

"Megan's fine."

"I'm so glad she's coming along okay," Sidney said sincerely. "I wondered if she'd be able to stay off her feet for such a long time, but she surprised me by acting so sensibly."

"You might consider doing the same," he said shortly, fumbling in a cabinet for a cup.

"Doing what?"

"Taking it easy. I know you're conscientious about this assignment, but don't you think you're overdoing it a little? You've been here until past eleven every night this week."

Beau grabbed the pot and filled his cup, setting it back with a clatter. *What was he doing!* For days he'd watched her engrossed in that computer, her mouth pursed in concentration, green eyes troubled one moment, puzzled the next, always searching. He silently cursed. He didn't want to have these feelings. He didn't want to notice the strain telling on her. Again, an instinct to protect her, to ease her responsibilities, struggled to be expressed, but he fought it down. He took a reckless swallow of the hot coffee, wincing. So why did that vulnerable look around her sweet mouth touch him? He looked away from her shadowed eyes. For no good reason, that was certain.

Sidney sipped her own coffee, making an effort to calm her senses. She hadn't missed the desire that had burned in Beau's eyes for a moment, so at odds with his attitude toward her. The man was a study in contradictions. She would give anything if she could simply convince herself she disliked him and be done with it. And she didn't delude herself that he was concerned for her welfare either. He probably suspected she was circumventing his orders to stay out of Rutledge business except where it directly concerned the loan.

"You don't have to be worried that I've violated the restrictions you set down," she said stiffly, her chin angled slightly upward.

Impatiently he set his cup down with a thump. "I know that! Actually—"

He bit off the rest of his reply at the ping of the microwave.

Sidney jerked at the glass door, relieved to do something with her hands. Caution forgotten, she reached in and took out the croissant, but the piping hot cream cheese oozed out and burned her fingers.

"Ouch!" She dropped the whole thing, reaching for something to wipe her hand.

"Here." Beau clamped her wrist with firm fingers and thrust her hand under the cold water tap. "You really aren't very domesticated, are you?" he snapped.

She tried to pull away, but he held her easily. "Just keep it under the water a minute and it won't be nearly as painful."

If Beau had been aware of her before, then he was ten times more so now. He groaned inwardly as his arm nestled firmly against her rib cage. Only the knit of her dress separated the soft outer curve of her breast and his arm. She was warm and gently rounded where her hip and thigh were molded to his. He was helplessly aware of her.

"Please, I'm fine," she choked, and made the mistake of sending an imploring look up at him just as he looked down at her. The moment was charged with the emotion they provoked in each other. Beau's eyes traveled recklessly over her face, seeing the gold-tipped lashes sweep down to screen her eyes. Irresistibly, he examined the enchanting curve of her cheek, the shape of her nose. Her hair curled in russet abandon along her temples.

He swayed a fraction of an inch closer, lured by her flowery scent and the age-old anticipation he saw in her eyes. Her lips parted invitingly and he was lost. He bent to claim her mouth.

"Morning, you two! Gorgeous day, isn't it?"

Beau and Sidney sprang apart guiltily on hearing Gail's voice. Sidney tore her gaze from the golden-eyed intensity of Beau's and plucked her hand out of his grasp.

"Morning, Gail," Beau said in a voice with a slightly rough edge. A shaken Sidney shut off the water and reached for a paper towel.

"Good morning, Gail," she said huskily, studiously avoiding the woman's shrewd gaze.

"Is it still stinging?" Beau asked, taking Sidney's hand again into his large one and examining it gently. Did she imagine it, or was his strong hand slightly unsteady?

"It's fine." Her scorched fingers were the least of her concerns. What in the world had just happened? Worse yet, what would have happened if Gail hadn't appeared when she did? He had nearly kissed her, and heaven help her, she had nearly let him. *Would* have let him.

She tugged her hand away, knowing how captivating Beau was when he was acting tender and concerned. Until half a minute ago, she'd believed she could resist his appeal, but she decided not to test her resistance just now.

"What happened?" Gail asked, darting a curious look at them.

Intent on escape, Sidney picked up her croissant and ducked around Beau's solid length. "The silliest thing," she said with a nervous laugh. "I got a little too close to hot cream cheese."

"And I was rendering first aid," Beau said, mocking her with a wicked gleam in his eyes.

"You be more careful next time," Gail cautioned, her look dwelling with interest on Sidney's flushed face.

"Yeah," Beau said solemnly. "That was close."
Sidney fled.

It was midmorning before she was fully in control again. Somehow, over the past few weeks, she'd managed to convince herself that she could accept this job and daily exposure to Beau Rutledge with the same cool poise that she'd maintained in other jobs. Beau's own cool detachment had added to her complacency. But that episode in the kitchen had shattered her illusions. Although she wanted to deny it, she was still strongly attracted to Beau, and to make matters a thousand times worse, it seemed that the initial attraction Beau had felt for her was still there.

She grimaced, dropping her forehead on one hand. This was awful! Beau was nothing like the kind of man she admired. But as much as she hated to admit it, he was the kind of man she was attracted to. She thought of the months in Atlanta when she'd dated Spencer. Why hadn't she fallen in love with him? He was thoughtful, kind, *predictable*. No dashing good looks or glib smiles, just sincere and dependable. Not hero material, but who needed that?

She groaned, getting up out of her chair and pacing around her office. If Beau was so unsuitable, then why did she have these crazy yearnings whenever she was close to him? She was no different from most women. She wanted to fall in love, marry, have children. But not with a man like Beau. Everything she knew about him should make him less appealing. He was a dangerous man. That is, he was dangerous if she was stupid enough to contemplate any kind of personal relationship with him. And she wasn't contemplating any such thing, she told herself sternly. There were plenty of other fish in the sea. One would come along.

Would you settle for Spencer Foley or Ted Lipscomb? a perverse little voice inside her head demanded. Oh Lord, could a woman have an exciting marriage without throwing in her lot with a man like Beau Rutledge?

When her telephone rang, she turned to glare at it, feeling too raw and unsettled to speak to anyone. But that was so... unprofessional. She sighed and answered it.

"Sid? This is Megan."

Great. Another Rutledge and one with almost as much appeal as Beau. "How are you, Megan?" she asked brightly. "Does it look like your ankle will be okay?"

"For cheerleader tryouts, you mean? Sure, it seems all right now, but I'm being extra careful to let it heal completely. I don't want a bum ankle to knock me out of the competition."

Sidney smiled wanly and stroked the side of her neck where tension and Beau Rutledge had tied a knot. "How's your grandmother, honey?"

"She's okay, I guess, and that's the reason I called, Sid."

Sidney braced herself. She recognized that tone from past skirmishes.

"Grammy is so lonely and depressed, Sid, and you know how people are when they get that way. They get in a rut and it's up to other people to do something about it."

"Sometimes, Megan," Sidney agreed cautiously.

"So, I thought I would do a little something to kind of cheer her up," Megan went on blithely. "Maybe have

a little get-together, something casual and uncompli-
cated. You know—not too many people. Fix something on the grill outdoors, say late in the afternoon.
What do you think about that, Sid?''

Sidney cleared her throat, thinking of the boisterous
atmosphere that would pervade any party with more
than a couple of Megan's friends. ''Sounds like a nice
idea so long as you keep it simple, honey. You don't
want to overwhelm your grandmother.''

''I knew you'd understand, Sid,'' Megan said happily. ''How does Sunday afternoon at four look on your
calendar?''

On my calendar. Sidney threw a helpless look around
her office. The last thing she wanted was to spend Sunday evening at Beau Rutledge's house.

Sunday. She searched her mind for a reasonable excuse to decline.

''Sidney? You're not thinking of saying no, are
you?''

Terrific. Her gaze fell on a memo Gail had stuck on
her calendar. Beau was scheduled to be in Chicago on
Monday. That meant he'd have to fly out Sunday. Sidney relaxed. As long as Beau was elsewhere, an evening
spent with Megan and Katherine Rutledge was appealing.

''I'm counting on you, Sid,'' Megan said on a plain-
tive note. ''Grammy likes you so much and you know
it wouldn't work for me to have a bunch of my friends
from school. You know how they *mean* well, Sid, but
they get kind of loud and they'll want to—''

Roped in and well aware of it, Sidney sighed. ''All
right, Megan. Sunday at four. I'll be there.''

There was a moment of silence at Megan's end. Then
a whispered, ''Thanks, Sidney,'' in a tone that com-

pletely belied the gleeful expression on the young girl's face as she hung up the phone.

"I guess you've heard from Megan by now."

At the sound of Beau's deep voice, Sidney looked up from the green display of her computer and commanded her heart to behave. She saw at a glance that he looked even more rakishly attractive now, hours after the kitchen episode. Apparently he'd been outdoors and his hair was an undisciplined sun-streaked mess. She watched him remove his sunglasses in a maneuver that was wholly masculine. It was when her gaze met his that she saw the challenge in his topaz eyes.

Her instinct was to run, especially when she knew his thoughts had leaped to meet hers, both recalling the earlier moment of near intimacy. But this time, she was going to stay in her chair behind her desk. Whatever he wanted could be dealt with over the comforting bulk of her trusty computer.

"She wants you to come over Sunday afternoon."

Sidney nodded. "I've spoken to her. I told her I would."

For a moment, satisfaction was the only reaction he displayed. Then he advanced, looking...uncertain? "I'll pick you up about quarter to four."

Dismay and surprise made her squeak, "Are you going to be there?"

"I live there."

She rolled her eyes impatiently. "I mean, don't you have to be on an airplane then?"

"I put the trip off for Megan."

"Well, couldn't you manage to have a date or something?"

The expression in his eyes turned cold. "I'm overwhelmed. If I'd only known how crazy you are about me, I'd have arranged this intimate little affair long ago," he said with biting sarcasm.

Agitated, she jumped to her feet. "You know what I mean!" She pushed at her ruffled auburn hair with an exasperated hand. Megan was matchmaking again! She flicked a glance at Beau's taut features. At least he was a victim, too. He couldn't be any more pleased than she was.

"Look," she said, injecting a "we're two adults she's a foolish child" note into her voice. "Megan let me assume this was a girl thing, an informal cookout to cheer up her grandmother. She knew I didn't expect you to be there." Sidney managed a wan smile. "No offense, but I don't want to go if you're there."

He leaned against the door a second, subjecting her to a silent unreadable look before reaching out and deliberately closing the door. Even with the span of her desk between them, Sidney found herself backing up, intimidated by the sheer breadth of him. And the look in his topaz eyes.

"No offense," he said softly, "but the feeling is mutual, lady."

"Don't call me that!" she snapped, and only sheer bravado held her upright. He was literally quivering with outrage. Or something. And Sidney hadn't a clue as to why. Did his niece's whims matter so much that he'd endure a whole evening in Sidney's company? She shot him another look. Had she wounded his ego? She tilted her head consideringly. A man like Rutledge? No way. Only with a Sherman tank.

"I think we both know how the other feels," Beau said with a strange inflection in his voice. It could have been anything—weariness, indifference. But regret? Pain? Surely not.

"Then why did you let her do it!" Sidney cried, panicked at the thought of being paired off with Beau under the gleeful eyes of a bunch of sixteen-year-olds. It would be dreadful! She and Beau could hardly exchange a civil word in spite of the inexplicable attraction that erupted at the strangest times.

"I didn't let her do it," he countered harshly. "I'm as much a victim as you. Besides, what difference does it make?"

"You know neither one of us wants to spend an evening together, for heaven's sake!" she cried, exasperated.

"Just be sure you don't let Megan discover that," Beau stated evenly, a threat implicit in his voice.

"I'd planned to work Sunday," she said more calmly. "I really don't have time for this."

"Make time," he ordered flatly. "Megan adores you." His tone clearly implied that he personally couldn't understand why. "She's lost both of her parents, for God's sake! Can't you put aside your precious career for one night?"

Sidney ground her teeth, defeated. Trust him, *the devil,* to hit upon the single fact that made it impossible for her to refuse Megan. He subjected her to one last searching look as though to satisfy himself that all her objections had been crushed. Then he was gone.

In a burst of frustration, Sidney paced around the confines of her office. Her eyes fell on the sunglasses, which he'd apparently forgotten. Impulsively, she swept up the leather case without a thought for the expensive lenses, relishing the satisfying thump it made as it bounced off the door.

Even so, she caught a quick apprehensive breath as Beau swiftly opened the door, his topaz eyes locking with hers in a telling look before he bent down to pick up the case. Without a word he stepped back and closed the door soundlessly.

Chapter Six

Sidney spent the next two days holed up in her office telling herself she needed the time to concentrate on the emerging pattern of discrepancies that was slowly but surely shaping up on the computer. The plain and simple truth, though, was that she was hiding from Beau.

It didn't do any good to tell herself that she would be able to handle this assignment the way she'd managed all other assignments she'd undertaken for the Peabody. No other assignment came with a man like Beau Rutledge. It already galled her that he knew he could destroy her composure. She was determined that he'd never have the satisfaction of knowing how appealing he was to her capricious heart. She was just going to have to squelch the renegade compulsion that had her fantasizing about him!

And so it seemed highly advisable to keep out of the way. No more of those bewitching encounters like the one in the kitchen. As for the wretched dinner date that

Megan had roped them into, well, she'd see that there were no more moments when she and Beau were alone. That shouldn't be too hard to manage with Megan and her grandmother right there. That left only the ride to the house and then back again. With a little luck, maybe she could even maneuver it so that Megan could drive her home.

By Friday night, she was feeling a little less threatened. Beau had been blessedly absent all day and she'd zipped through the routine tasks of her job before tackling the one that really intrigued her. The hours had sped by as she methodically analyzed the information that was stored in the computer, all of her detective instincts on red alert. She scowled deeply at the display. She was so close to uncovering whatever system was being used to manipulate the computer!

Drained, she massaged her tight temples. Quitting time was long past, but the baffling information only made her more determined. Her job had not been easy considering the continuing lack of cooperation from Beau's staff.

With a final contemplative frown, Sidney leaned back, almost bleary-eyed from the intense concentration of the past hours. It didn't seem as though she would solve the puzzle tonight. Her neck was stiff, her back ached, and it had been so long since she had last eaten that her appetite had come and gone. She didn't know what time it was, only that it was well after midnight.

She yawned widely and stretched, rubbing the tension in her neck. No sense spending any more time working tonight. Her concentration was disappearing quickly under the combined forces of fatigue and hunger. She opened a drawer and raked pencils, paper clips and yellow highlighter inside, then collected the paper that littered her desk top and slipped the sheets neatly into the drawer. For a moment, she just sat, eyes closed, the tips of her fingers kneading the burning muscle where her neck joined her shoulder.

"Do you know what time it is, woman!"

Sidney nearly jumped out of her skin as Beau's voice thundered, shattering the total silence of the deserted office along with Sidney's composure.

Before she recovered enough presence of mind to reply, he rushed on. "What do you think you're doing at—" he sliced a furious glance at his watch "—two-thirty in the morning? I know you throw everything you've got into your job, Sidney, but this is ridiculous. It's more than ridiculous, it's stupid! No one needs to put in this kind of time for a job!"

Sidney rose slowly, her face vulnerable, and stared at him for a moment. "Is it that late?" she asked blankly. He'd called her Sidney, and even as she thought it, a part of her—the renegade part, the side of her that was attracted to him—responded with the usual rush of awareness and leaping pulse. Dazedly she wondered if he thought of her as Sidney and not the Ms. James that he always called her. Did he have a few renegade impulses, too?

"Am I going to get an answer?" he demanded, his tall broad frame filling the doorway.

"I was tracking some numbers that came out of the number three mill," she explained with forced patience. "The one that's near West Helena."

He gave her an exasperated look. "I know where the number three mill is, Sidney. Was it enough to keep you here more than eight hours after everyone else has gone? And on a Friday night, no less!"

Tired as she was, Sidney knew she was no match for Beau. When she did reveal her suspicions to him—if she ever did—she wanted all the pieces of the puzzle. In Beau's own words, she wanted all the *i*'s dotted and the *t*'s crossed. And she was a long way from that. So right now, she'd have to fob him off somehow.

The smile she attempted wobbled a little. "You know how it is with us accountants," she quipped as casually as she could manage. "We hate to leave if the numbers don't balance. But I'd just decided to wrap it up when you appeared." She turned off her computer and stepped around her desk. "And since you mentioned it first, why are you here?"

He moved aside, allowing her to slip through the door before pulling it closed and falling into step beside her. "I was on my way home and saw the light in your office. I couldn't believe even you would take a job that seriously. Don't you have any personal life at all?"

She sighed, turning into a long hall that led away from the office complex through an area that served as temporary storage space. Retail merchandise was stacked in bins on both sides of the hallway. At this time of night, it was shadowy and still. Sidney increased her pace slightly, not wanting to linger in the dim deserted region with Beau. Or was it that she wanted too much to linger with this man? a small inner voice mocked.

Agitated by his proximity and her own thoughts, Sidney failed to notice a stack of wood piled on a cart that was pushed flush against the wall bins. She passed by quickly, but her skirt pocket caught on a long piece that was sticking out and she was jerked to a halt. Wide-eyed, she watched as the whole display shifted.

"Sidney!"

Seconds after she heard the harsh alarm in Beau's voice she was flung to the floor, pinned beneath his strong solid body. She squeezed her eyes closed, turning her face into his neck, and braced for the impact. She heard the clatter of the wood as the whole display collapsed and fell. It took a moment for Sidney to realize that she wasn't buried beneath the debris. Instead, she was buried beneath Beau. All six feet plus of bone and sinew was sprawled protectively over her. His mouth was at her ear. She could hear the rasp of his breath and the muffled oath as the wood rained down around them.

They were still for a minute, and then Beau stirred. One leg had been thrown intimately over her to shield her lower limbs and the rest of her was cocooned in the cradle of his arms. He lifted his head a fraction from her ear. "Are you hurt?" he managed, his voice tense. She felt the taut anxiety in his body as she stirred experimentally.

"I don't think so."

He sagged against her in relief. "You could have been," he said roughly. "I don't know who was responsible for leaving that booby trap right in the middle of the hall, but I'll know by morning!"

Sidney's laugh had a shaky sound. "It was my own fault. I wasn't watching where I was going." She stirred again, steeling herself against the pervading warmth that washed over her at the feel of his hard thighs fitted intimately against her.

He was suddenly still, looking down at her. "Most of it missed us," he said thickly. Her hair was fanned out in a russet tangle that framed her delicate features. His gaze slid over her face, watching the elusive light catch in her hair and cast shadows that etched the hollows of her cheekbones and darkened the fringe of her lashes. The emerald of her eyes was almost black. Her unintentional dishevelment was more provocative than anything she could have done by design.

Beau was captivated.

What she saw in his dark gaze made her turn away with a softly protesting sound. Sidney's heart began a slow dull throb. Caught by a feeling that was utterly feminine, she was acutely aware of Beau's weight on her, heavy and seductive. Helplessly, her gaze fell on one muscled arm braced at her cheek. He was tanned and strong, his forearm liberally dusted with tawny hair, gold-tipped from the sun. Time was suspended as she studied his hand, seeing him flex his long fingers. She liked his hands, imagining how they would feel exploring the secrets of her body. Two weeks ago that thought would have shocked her, but now it only intensified the desire that was already threatening to burst into flames between them.

In mute fascination, her eyes journeyed upward, taking in the sheer masculinity of his broad shoulders. She stared entranced at the throbbing pulse at the base of his throat.

More golden-brown hair curled provocatively at the opening of his shirt and her stomach clenched at the sight of it. She drew a deep shuddering breath, trying to control her rioting senses, but succeeded only in intoxicating herself with the scent of his after-shave that mixed sensually with the musky male smell of the man himself.

Their eyes met and lingered, hers wide and green, his smoky amber and steadily darkening with growing desire. Fierce need streaked through Sidney and suddenly she knew what it meant to want a man.

"I must get up," she murmured, her heartbeat thundering in her ears, fighting the languor that swamped her. Breathless and still, she watched as he bent to her mouth.

"We can't do this," she whispered, the tiny objection issued against his hovering lips. His breath was soft and cool, faintly tinged with bourbon. *Was he drunk?* "This is crazy...."

"Yes, crazy," he muttered, his lips just touching the corner of her mouth. "Crazy," he repeated, his tongue tracing the soft outline of her lips ever so slowly. "But if I don't do this, I'll go crazy," he groaned thickly, and then he took her mouth in a total devastating kiss.

She couldn't remember putting her arms around his neck, or when his full weight resettled against her softness. Her mouth parted involuntarily, eagerly, to his and then they were both caught up in the passion that exploded between them.

Sidney had told herself over and over that there had been nothing particularly special about that first kiss they'd exchanged at the bank party. She'd tried to convince herself that her memory had enhanced the embrace with more pleasure than there had actually been. But now, swamped by the taste of him, the smell of him, she knew her imagination hadn't erred. It was even better than she'd allowed herself to remember, and all of her senses were alive and reveling in rediscovery.

Restraint and denial were forgotten as his tongue explored her lips, entreating until she yielded, then plunged to recklessly claim the sweet depths beyond. Sidney, swallowing a small inarticulate sound, responded with a shy thrust of her tongue that wrenched a murmur of satisfaction from Beau. He caught her face

between his palms, indulging them both in a heady
erotic feast.

When they were forced to break apart, gasping for
breath, his mouth rushed over her face, nuzzling under
the curve of her jaw, finding the throb of her pulse at
the hollow of her throat and lingering to savor it.

Chemistry. What was happening here was only
chemistry, Sidney reasoned weakly, although she certainly wasn't being governed by reason at the moment.
Instead, she felt driven by that wild compulsion she'd
denied for too long. It had finally burst into full-fledged
passion. And from the fervor she sensed in Beau, he
must be feeling it, too.

His hands swept along the line of her thighs, up past
her waist and over the swell of her breasts. Quickly his
fingers dispensed with the buttons of her silk blouse,
and when his palm cupped her breast, Sidney drew in a
sharp breath that seemed to fuel his desire. He returned to her mouth and swallowed up her little cry with
another kiss. Silk and lace were swept aside as he found
her nipples and with his thumbs gently coaxed the tiny
buds to hard tight buttons of desire.

Sidney's hands groped for his head, plunging her
fingers deeply into his hair and then guided him recklessly to that which yearned for his touch. When his lips
closed on one tip, she moaned, murmuring something
neither of them understood.

Nothing had ever seemed so urgent and so necessary
as the loving stroke of his tongue along the slope of her
breast. Her whole body trembled and as though he
understood her fear and need, he murmured gentle
words, soothing the throbbing dusky center without
haste, savoring the satin delicacy of her skin.

The slam of the huge metal door of the warehouse stunned them both. Sidney froze, then was catapulted into action at the sound of heavy footsteps. Almost panicked, she pushed at Beau, who responded like a man drugged. His movements were thick and uncoordinated as he rolled sideways, giving his head a dull shake as though clearing it after a stunning blow.

Sidney scrambled to her feet and turned away to clip her bra and do up the buttons of her blouse. Mortified, she swept the fiery cloud of her hair away from her face and clamped her jaw resolutely. She had to face him, but nothing in her experience had prepared her for a situation like this.

"You folks burnin' the midnight oil, eh, Mr. Rutledge?"

Beau turned his hooded gaze from Sidney's rose-tinted profile reluctantly. "Right, Kelly. Ms. James and I were just on our way out when we tangled with a display that was illegally parked." Casually, he moved so that Sidney was shielded from the night watchman's eyes. When the man bent to begin clearing the debris, Beau stopped him.

"You don't have to bother picking this up tonight. Head on around to the front of the building, Kelly, and make your usual rounds. We'll clear a path here and then go out the back way."

Sidney's breathing was still uneven and her hands shaking, but as the night watchman ambled away and was swallowed up in the gloom, she braced herself to face Beau.

When he turned, she saw that he looked as stunned as she felt. His unique amber eyes were dark and unreadable as they swept up to hers. A short potent silence hovered between them, then they both rushed into speech.

"I didn't—"

"That wasn't—"

Beau slashed a frustrated hand through his hair, the gesture more eloquent than a hundred words would have been. "What were you saying?"

Sidney caught up a folder, hugging it against her chest, and shrugged dismissively. "Nothing important. I think I'll let you tidy up. These long hours are about to catch up with me." She eyed him warily when he said nothing. "Well, good night."

She took a step and halted. Where was her purse?

"Are you sure you weren't hurt? I came down pretty hard on you."

"I'm okay." She spotted her purse under the wood and stole another uneasy glance at him, looking away when he did the same. He began shoving aside some of the debris. She bent to lift a length that was wedged across the aisle.

"That was a mistake."

She dropped the wood and threw him a startled look.

"Not the wood. The kiss."

"For once we agree," she said curtly, well aware of his opinion of her as a woman, but perversely not wanting to be reminded so bluntly about it. "It was chemistry, nothing else."

His bronzed brows shot upward. "Chemistry?"

She took in a long patient breath. "I'm a woman and you're a man. It's late, and we're both tired."

Contrarily, instead of accepting her pat explanation of the explosive passion they'd just shared, Beau grinned. "I think that scenario is supposed to result in the opposite reaction. In case you missed it, we both went up in flames ten minutes ago.''

She frowned, suddenly uneasy again.

''But you were right about one thing,'' he said with a return of the cool detachment that was so familiar to her.

She gave him a questioning look.

''It was chemistry. Nothing else.''

''Just one of those things,'' she agreed grimly, determined not to let him know how devastating those minutes had been to her. Inwardly she was a seething mass of confusion and bewilderment. Why did her capricious body respond so wantonly to him? She hesitated, torn between an urgent need to run away and a purely female craving to provoke him. She stared into his eyes, finding them bright with challenge.

''You don't have to be so eager to fly, little bird,'' he mocked, accurately sizing up her intent. ''It won't happen again.''

''It sure won't,'' she muttered, bending to pick up her shoulder bag.

''I don't want to get involved with a woman who is married to a computer,'' he informed her, but she noticed an irritated edge to his words that robbed them of some of their conviction.

She sighed and shifted the folder, settling her shoulder strap firmly. She was well aware how much Beau resented having her on his territory every day, but so far his good manners had prevented an open show of contempt. It surprised her how much his contempt hurt. She hung on to her composure with an effort when all she wanted to do was burst into tears. Instead she lifted her chin and eyed him disdainfully.

"I'll keep that in mind if I ever decide that I want to get involved with you, Mr. Rutledge," she said, her words low and trembling. "But as difficult as it may be for you to believe, hell will freeze over before I would ever wish to get involved with the likes of you!"

For a split second, Beau drew in a sharp breath. He even winced a little—or did she imagine that? But she didn't imagine his short mirthless laugh. "I guess you'd reject an apology—"

"In a New York minute!" Sidney snapped, pivoting away in a graceful arc, her hair flaring out in a fiery cloud. "Good night," she said with glacial politeness and stalked off, her russet head high.

Congratulations, Rutledge. You handled that with all the finesse of an ape at a garden party! Disgusted, Beau slammed an armload of wood haphazardly onto the aisle cart and dusted off his hands. He'd really ripped it with her now.

He strode impatiently down the deserted aisle and slammed the big metal door of the warehouse just as Sidney's Rabbit was shooting out of the parking lot. He muttered something vile before stalking to the Blazer.

Great. Terrific. Two-thirty in the morning and she's striking out alone on some of Memphis's most disreputable streets. He pulled out with a screech of the Blazer's tires, knowing he'd been wise not to suggest that she might need a man to accompany her. She'd really scream male chauvinist then. But in spite of the fact that she considered herself an independent woman, it was still the middle of the night. Any woman was vulnerable at that hour.

He shifted restlessly, propping an elbow on the open window and leaning his head wearily on one fist. Why did he even care? That lady could probably whip her weight in wildcats. She sure gave as good as she got in a tangle with him. He groaned again, feeling disgusted and more than a little remorseful for making that stupid remark about not getting involved with a woman married to a computer.

Add another to a growing list of dumb things he'd said lately. Like telling her he didn't want to be around if she was going to Megan's party. It was a bald-faced lie. Even though he knew she wanted to avoid him, he was drawn to her more than any woman he'd ever met. Any woman.

Beau cursed impatiently. She had him reacting like a teenager. When she'd said that she didn't want to go if he was there, he'd retaliated without thinking. He couldn't remember when a woman had had the power to hurt him.

Frustrated, he raked his hand through his hair. He had to keep reminding himself how wrong she was for him. Hadn't he had enough of women who gave the best of themselves to a job? What kind of fool was he to still want her? He smothered another oath. All he knew was that he did want her.

He kept discovering new facets of her that intrigued him, that made him question his original assessment of her as a woman blindly dedicated to her career. Just a few days ago, he'd come in from a business lunch and, as had been his habit from day one, he'd glanced in her office only to find it empty. He'd immediately gone in search of Gail to satisfy his curiosity.

"She got a call from a woman at a day-care center," Gail explained. "She said she wouldn't be back until tomorrow."

Beau frowned, looking puzzled. "A day-care center?"

Gail spread her hands wide and shrugged. "Apparently her friend, Jill, coaches a gymnastics team and is out of town for an afternoon competition. Jill's little boy developed a temperature at the day-care center and they called Sidney. She explained that she's the person they call in an emergency if Jill isn't available."

Beau bent his head, making a pretense of sifting through some papers on Gail's desk. "A pretty unlikely substitute mother, huh?"

He felt rather than saw Gail's quick glance. "Are we talking about the same lady here?" she replied in obvious surprise. Her manner became overly patient as though explaining something to a slow learner. "Beau, Sidney's a pushover for kids, pets and old ladies. She's got a marshmallow heart, that one. Haven't you ever noticed how she treats Megan? And your mother? Jill relies on her, too, being a single parent and all. I think she's Josh's godmother."

Beau shuffled a few pages, thinking wryly that it hadn't taken Gail long to fall victim to Sidney's charm. Could he be wrong? "You may be right," he said smoothly, but his mouth took a cynical slant. "As long as the demands of her career aren't affected. I can't see her letting anything come before that."

Gail studied him with a bland expression in her eyes, her head tipped to one side. "Well, she rushed out of here this afternoon acting more like a concerned parent than a dedicated workaholic. In fact, she made a quick call to Louis Maynard at the bank to cancel an appointment with him and a couple of the Peabody's directors. Something to do with a special assignment, I think she said. Sounded to me like Mr. Maynard insisted the meeting was important and her absence inconvenient. She was apologetic, but firm. She told him Josh needed her.''

Beau gazed into the dark Tennessee night. Canceling an important meeting at the bank and running to the aid of a little boy didn't exactly fit his impression of Sidney. Thoughtfully he scraped his hand over his face, frowning as he attempted to keep his mind on the road. Not only had he insulted Sidney, but he'd probably hurt her when he'd fallen on her. But, God help him, there had been no way he could have stopped himself from kissing her. He'd wanted to kiss her in the kitchen three days ago. And probably would have if Gail hadn't walked in. Just as he'd probably have ravished her tonight if old Kelly hadn't blundered in.

Keeping the winking red taillights of her Rabbit in sight, he felt something deep inside him tighten and then begin an aching throb. In his mind he conjured up the image of her tousled hair and kiss-softened lips. He shook his head in wonder. He was spending a lot of time thinking about Ms. Sidney James. Everything about her appealed to him except her single-mindedness about her career. He didn't think he could handle that problem again.

So why not an affair, a cynical voice reasoned in his head. But something told him that Sidney was an all or nothing type of woman. Besides, he had a feeling that a short-term relationship with Sidney would be highly unsatisfactory. He wasn't at all certain he could walk away when the time came.

Chapter Seven

Sidney fumbled and slapped at the snooze bar of her alarm clock several times before it dawned on her that it was her telephone ringing. She groaned and groped for the receiver, flopping back against a pillow, semiconscious.

"Sidney? Did I wake you up?"

Her eyes flew open, every nerve suddenly wideawake.

"This is Beau. Sidney? Hello?"

Of course it was. She'd know that deep, rough-edged voice anywhere in the whole world. "Hello."

His wry chuckle danced over her nerve endings and set her senses humming.

"I did wake you. I'm sorry." He hesitated a second and when she said nothing, "Look, I'll call back in a couple of hours. You—"

"No! Um, I mean, it's time I was up anyway." She flicked a glance at her clock radio. Nine-seventeen. "It's okay."

"I thought I might miss you if I waited much longer," he said, a note of misgiving making him sound strangely boyish.

Sidney struggled up higher against her pillow into a sitting position. "What did you—" Then it occurred to her that Beau wouldn't call her about anything except Megan. "Is Megan hurt?" she asked quickly.

"No, no. It's not Megan." He gave a husky half laugh, and again the sound shivered over Sidney's nerve ends. "I wanted to remind you that today is Sunday—Megan's party, remember? I'll pick you up a few minutes before four this afternoon."

"Oh."

"You haven't decided not to come, have you, Sidney?"

Sidney idly twirled the phone cord. "No, of course not. I promised her I would."

"I thought you might reconsider after what happened Friday night."

Sidney blinked at the bar of sunshine streaming through her window. A warmth that had nothing to do with the sun tingled all the way to her toes. All the considering in the world hadn't managed to banish the feel of his hands and the taste of his mouth. Or the crazy hunger for more of the same. "That had nothing to do with Megan," she said huskily.

"I was hoping you would feel that way."

There was a short pause.

"Well, I'll see you around four," she said, her fingers tight around the receiver for some reason.

"You didn't work yesterday."

"I don't work on Saturday, Beau."

Another pause. "You've never said that before," he replied, his voice deeper than ever.

She laughed softly. "I'd work on Saturday if it became necessary, but—"

He interrupted her with a low sound. "I mean you've never said my name." He waited before adding gruffly, "I like the sound of it."

A heady excitement curled inside Sidney. The cord lay still and forgotten in her fingers. She was thankful this conversation was not face-to-face so he couldn't see the effect his words had on her. She glanced down at her sheer nightgown. Her breasts were tight, pouting against the silk. Even her body was flushed! *Face it, Sidney James,* she told her galloping heart, *you are putty in this man's hands whether you want to admit it or not.*

"I tried to reach you yesterday to apologize."

"Apologize?"

"For making that stupid remark about your being married to your computer. You probably have me figured as Memphis's most pigheaded chauvinist." Even on the phone, she could hear the note of disgust in his words. "But I'd like to hear you say you forgive me anyway. Would you, Sidney?"

She smiled, unable to resist his appeal. "Okay."

"But not the kiss."

Sidney's heart dipped. For a split second, she'd been close to forgetting the kind of man she was dealing with. *Now,* she told herself, now was the time to say something sophisticated and cool, except that nothing like that came to mind. What did come to mind was the delicious recollection of that kiss he wasn't going to apologize for.

When the silence again stretched between them, he took it for acquiescence. "Thanks," he said softly. And in the background Sidney could hear someone call out to him. He muffled the receiver and called something before getting back to her. "I've got to run, sw—uh, Sidney; Megan's threatening to leave me at the mercy of Stacey and Melanie at the cookout this afternoon if I don't wrap this up."

Sidney knew just how merciless teenage girls could be toward any hapless male they admired, and she chuckled. Then before she could stop herself, "Where are you and Megan going so early on a Sunday?"

She could almost hear his grin. "C'mon, think," he chided. "Sunday at the Rutledge house? Where else? Megan and I are going to church with Mother."

While Sidney was still considering that, she heard Megan's impatient voice again and Beau's knowing grunt. "I bet she'd let us be late without a whimper if she knew who I was talking to," he said with a wicked laugh. Then his voice dropped to a low intimate tone. "See you at four."

Sidney replaced the receiver with fingers that weren't quite steady. Why did Beau turn her emotions upside down? She made an impatient noise and fell back on her pillow. On Friday night he'd insinuated that she didn't quite measure up as a woman. Now he expected a glib apology to erase that hurt and anger. She chewed her inside lip, staring at the ceiling fan that revolved lazily over her bed. Why did she respond from her deepest, most feminine core to Beau's masculine appeal? Her green eyes had a faraway look. She thought of his indulgence to Megan. Apparently his good nature even extended to accompanying his mother and Megan to church. A rosy warmth spread through her and brought a smile to her lips. It took a moment for her to realize just how totally he'd managed to change her attitudes. Like a ninny, she was ready to forgive him for every transgression she suspected him of.

With a quick impatient sigh, Sidney tossed the sheet aside and slid out of bed. How could she be thinking like this! Why did her silly heart persist in weaving ridiculous fantasies about Beau? With a briskness that was calculated to banish those fantasies, she forced her imagination in line and turned on the shower. Lisa Rutledge had probably endowed Beau with a lot of sterling qualities, too, and just look at the way that turned out. The man was a *devil*!

And, for heaven's sake, had she forgotten the computer scam? She hadn't proven anything yet, but her investigation had detected enough information to convince her it was just a matter of time before she uncovered some specifics.

She yanked the curtain aside and stepped into the shower. So why didn't she feel more satisfaction, she demanded of her foolish heart. She turned the faucet to cold and submitted to the bracing spray with a dejected air.

Beau knew the moment Sidney opened the door that the sweetly enchanting woman who'd talked to him on the phone that morning was gone. *Probably stormed her defenses while she was half-asleep,* he concluded, and made a wry mental note to remember it. He knew he'd have no trouble conjuring up a picture of her as she'd probably been that morning—tousled, sleepy, warm—in short, breathtakingly sexy.

"All ready?" he asked with a smile. Not that she wasn't sexy right now. His eyes made a lightning quick tour of her in canary-yellow shirt and crisp white shorts. He knew better than to let his eyes linger. But it was hard. Time for that later after he'd done his best to banish that dangerous glint in her green eyes.

"Just let me get my bag," she said coolly, turning to collect a canvas tote, and giving him a view of her adorable rear end and the best-looking legs he'd ever seen.

He cleared his throat and attempted to clear the vivid images that flooded into his overstimulated imagination. With a polite touch of his hand to the small of her back, he escorted her to his car.

"Megan is looking forward to this," he said, feeling that his niece was bound to be a subject they could agree on. He opened the door and refrained from touching her.

"That's the only reason I'm here," Sidney said, letting him know beyond doubt that her mellow mood was a thing of the past.

He closed the door with a resigned sigh and rounded the hood. Back to square one. He climbed into the car and congratulated himself on letting her remark pass unchallenged. It was going to take some diplomacy to bring her around. "Does this mean the truce is over?" he asked lightly.

She turned her gaze away, giving him a view of a delicately obstinate jaw and chin. "What truce? You know you didn't choose my company tonight any more than I chose yours. This whole wretched thing is Megan's idea. So I don't see the point in you or I pretending otherwise. Especially when we're alone."

With a wry arch of his brows, Beau let that pass too. Thoughtfully, he pinched his bottom lip with his thumb and forefinger, eyes straight ahead. This was a woman to be handled with finesse, he counseled himself, not bludgeoning tactics. He couldn't go with his instincts, although for a few heady moments he toyed with the fantasy of catching her up against him, tilting her mouth to his and kissing her bad temper away.

Fat chance. No, that was not the way to Ms. Sidney James's good graces. The tension between them was so explosive that the tiniest spark set them off. It baffled him. How were they going to spend the evening under the eagle eyes of Megan and her friends and still manage to hide the emotion that sizzled between them?

"I'm here because of Megan," Sidney said aloofly. "If I weren't obligated, there's no way I would have agreed to this."

Stung, Beau's good intentions disappeared. As his temper heated, his voice became more controlled. "I get the message," he said evenly, stunned to discover that she had the power to hurt him so much. "Just remember that Megan looks up to you," he said in instant retaliation. "I expect you to set a good example for her even though you might find it difficult, considering she's my niece."

At her quick look, his eyes held hers. "You haven't made your dislike of me any secret."

She bridled instantly, but wasn't given a chance to speak.

"I won't allow you to hurt Megan. For some reason she thinks you're wonderful."

Sidney's eyes flashed dangerously. "Look who's talking!" she burst out, throwing discretion to the winds. "You may have your poor mother *and* Megan *and* all your employees fooled, but you haven't got me fooled, *Mr. Clean*. I lived in Atlanta when you were there. Your divorce and the reason for it were all over town.''

Beau whipped over to the curb and slammed on the brakes. He turned to her with a ferocious scowl. ''Just what do you know about my divorce?'' he demanded.

Sidney nearly blanched under the searing look, realizing too late that she'd gone too far. How was she going to get out of this without revealing her connection with the Thompson Agency? Would he believe she'd picked up her information from gossip?

''I don't know any details,'' she admitted reluctantly, ''but it was common knowledge that you and your secretary were having—'' she hesitated as his eyes slitted menacingly ''—a relationship.''

Beau was still as stone.

''Your wife named your secretary in the divorce proceedings,'' Sidney offered weakly.

''Common knowledge.''

She sent him a quick look, uneasily noting the quiet dangerous quality about him. ''Can you deny it?'' she countered, but with far less confidence than before. He didn't look like a man who had anything to be ashamed of.

''I didn't know you lived in Atlanta,'' he said evenly.

She glanced down at her hands and found them tightly laced. She quickly relaxed them. ''There was no reason you should.''

''And there's no reason I should explain my personal life to you,'' he replied coldly. ''But after you hear me out, you can decide whether to believe me or not.'' He was openly contemptuous.

She threw out a hand. ''Look, I'm not—''

He swore, biting off something that Sidney knew would have scorched her ears. As it was, it silenced her abruptly.

"My 'relationship' as you referred to it was completely innocent. Amy was the unsuspecting victim in a situation that I would like to forget. She was engaged to my business partner, Will Baxter. Lisa, my wife, was the one having the affair, and it was with Baxter. But it was hardly love."

Some of the fury seemed to leave him, and his voice became deeper. "Maybe I could have understood it if she and Baxter had been in the throes of a deep love," Beau said with a mirthless half laugh. He gazed past Sidney to the dark street beyond. "But Lisa didn't really love anything except...achieving. She channeled all her energy and passion into her career.

"We met when we were co-workers for LTK, an international construction firm. She was very beautiful and I guess I was dazzled by the irresistible combination of brains and beauty. I now know that Lisa didn't love anyone or anything as much as she loved success. When we broke away from LTK to start our own business, she was thrilled. She threw herself into that with even more enthusiasm. Will Baxter was dazzled too, poor devil. She seduced him after she'd figured out a way to have it all."

"Please," Sidney protested, wishing fervently that she'd never mentioned Atlanta. She had a horrible feeling that she hadn't heard the worst yet.

"She broke up Will's engagement to Amy. Then on trumped-up charges she'd managed to get from some sleazy private detective, she tried to put the screws to me in the divorce settlement so she could marry Will. That way, she planned to get her share of the business, Will's share and most of mine."

He was quiet then, leaving Sidney dazed with horror. Sleazy detective. Oh, Lord. What had she done?

She darted a quick look at him, but he seemed not to notice. His eyes were dark with old pain. One shoulder was hunched over the steering wheel. His other arm was extended along the back of the seat, this hand nearly touching Sidney's hair. She had a crazy impulse to turn her cheek, rest it against his hand, offer...something.

He laughed shortly, without humor. "I went there later and actually used some of the material they'd compiled in a counterclaim to salvage my business."

"Went where?" she asked weakly.

"The Thompson Agency," he said derisively. "As spying goes, they're the best, or so I'm told."

"Oh."

He slanted distracted fingers through his hair, his gaze fastened on something in the distance. "Well, anyway, the one who'd worked up most of the material was gone, they said."

She should have known. Why hadn't she called them? Why hadn't she followed up when her instincts had told her she didn't have the whole story?

"I'm surprised they opened their files," she ventured.

Another short laugh. "I convinced them after a pretty heavy scene that their information had one fatal flaw. Lisa had carefully leaked exactly what she wanted known and then, when she got the results she wanted, she shut them off. It only took one run of the computer to convince them."

To save her life, Sidney couldn't think of a word to say.

"Those were hard times for Amy," Beau went on, still mired in his past. "For me too. Even though I didn't love Lisa, I wasn't immune to the pain of betrayal. Since Amy and I had both been jilted, well, you know what they say, misery loves company. It was totally innocent. Besides, I was really worried about Amy for a while."

His eyes cleared, found hers. That gold-brown gaze was intense, trying to tell her something. But she was beyond interpreting Beau's look. She was too busy surveying the extent of the damage she'd unintentionally done to this man. Again, she deplored the circumstances that had caused her to drop the case with too many unfinished aspects. And now that Beau had filled in the blanks, she was horrified. Horrified that she'd unwittingly handed Lisa Rutledge the weapon to destroy her marriage, to cast doubt on Beau's reputation and although he hadn't admitted it, he'd probably been ruined financially as well. Sidney almost groaned out loud at the results of her handiwork.

"Was any of that common knowledge?" Beau asked with scorn, drawing another wince from Sidney.

She forced herself to withstand the accusation in his eyes. "It's my turn to apologize," she said with as much dignity as she could muster. "I had no business mentioning your private life. Absolutely none. If you want to take me back, I will try to come up with some excuse that will pacify Megan."

A pair of topaz eyes held hers captive a long time. "Very sweetly said," he murmured finally.

A soft summer wind swept through a stand of cottonwoods just beyond the car. It teased Sidney's hair through the open window, lifting it gently. A silk strand caught on her mouth, and Beau reached out with one finger and guided it along her cheek, tucking the curl into the flamelike mass that lay on her shoulders. How would she ever keep him from finding out how much reason he had to despise her? she agonized, nearly collapsing with relief when he finally turned and started the car.

Chapter Eight

That's why you were so cold and standoffish with me from the start, wasn't it?''

Sidney pushed a piece of grilled steak around her plate, then forced herself to bite into it, her body fully aware of Beau's knees nestling against her bare thighs on the redwood bench. He'd settled astride it the moment the girls had jumped into the pool, making short work of Sidney's efforts to avoid any moments alone with him.

Sidney threw a quick concerned look at Katherine Rutledge, who was relaxed in a lounge enjoying Megan and her friends. She was too far away to be of any help to Sidney.

"Mother can't rescue you, Sidney." His voice was low enough so that no one could hear except Sidney. "Even though you were just as attracted as I was, you denied your feelings because of gossip and innuendo you picked up in Atlanta."

Sidney speared a radish and bit into it. "Is it so hard to understand?" she said, her voice harsh and low. "Why would I encourage a man who I knew had cheated on his wife? Besides, aren't you the one who said you'd stopped thinking of me as a woman?" Her eyes were accusing. "You saw me as a computer instead of a woman, wasn't that what you said?"

He set his glass down with a blunt thud and caught her chin in his hand. "I think we should talk about that—" He swore impatiently when the cordless phone at his elbow rang.

"Rutledge!" he growled into it, his gaze never leaving Sidney. He listened, then his tone mellowed. "Oh, she's right here." His amber eyes lazily roamed Sidney's face as he spoke into the phone. "Yes ma'am, you too." He leaned close and Sidney's heart thumped alarmingly. But just as he neared her mouth, he veered slightly to lean around her and call Katherine. "Mother, Miss Lorraine Spann wants to talk to you."

Flustered, Sidney's eyes fell to her plate while she forced herself to calm down. She'd thought for a split second that he was going to kiss her right in front of them all!

"Sidney!" Megan's cheery demand brought Sidney's head up. "Did you bring a swimsuit?"

Sidney managed a smile and shook her head.

"No problem," the irrepressible Megan said. "We're the same size and I've got one you can use. Come on in, both of you. The water's great," she pleaded when she saw Sidney didn't look as though she was going to cooperate.

"Yeah," Beau growled in her ear. "Anything to keep us from having two private minutes."

Sidney hesitated, weighing the options. The pool offered a respite from Beau's determined interrogation. She didn't want to talk about her feelings toward him. She *couldn't* talk about her feelings. He was too shrewd, too...compelling. One careless word and he might discover her connection with the agency.

She jumped up, for once falling in enthusiastically with Megan's machinations. "You're right, Meggie, a swim sounds great. Where's that suit?"

"What suit!" Five minutes later in the tiny cabana, Sidney surveyed herself in dismay. Megan's generosity had produced a crocheted scrap that wouldn't pass for a swimsuit in any civilized country. She tilted her head critically. The tiny cinnamon bikini was perfect for her, setting off the ivory of her long shapely limbs and the fiery highlights of her hair. Desperately she looked around for a cover-up. Nothing, naturally, not even a towel. She tugged at the backside of the bikini. She couldn't stay in here for the rest of the night, although that thought was the only reassuring one she'd had. At least in the dark he wouldn't be able to see so much of her.

"Hey, in there!"

Although he didn't yell, Sidney jumped at the sound of Beau's voice. She, who had never felt the slightest self-consciousness about her body, who had danced in a revealing leotard and less since she was three years old, had to breathe a deep restorative breath before she could bring herself to step outside.

But then, one look at Beau and her inhibitions vanished. He caught her hand and casually pulled her to the poolside, but not before she'd seen the quick flare in his eyes. She pushed away from him, took three running steps and dived into the water, but even with her eyes closed, she had no trouble seeing his lean, tanned, perfectly symmetrical body. His chest was covered with tawny hair that narrowed to a silken line on his flat stomach, then disappeared into dark green trunks. He was beautiful.

Beau was right behind her in the pool. She felt the force of the drive and the pull of the water as he stayed close but submerged. Ignoring him, she swam strongly, thrilled and threatened at once, her emotions adding to the impetus of her flight. Only when she'd stopped, panting, did she see that Megan was climbing out of the pool looking at her grandmother.

"Grammy," Megan wailed, grabbing a towel and slinging it around her shoulders. "This is all my fault! I forgot to tell you Miss Lorraine called you last week to make a fourth for bridge tonight. I'm sorry, Grammy. Is she very upset?"

Katherine Rutledge's genteel features had a distressed look. "Oh dear, Megan, how could you forget? Lorraine has two other guests and naturally they need a fourth. They were counting on me," she said in gentle admonishment.

Undaunted, Megan blotted water from her curly mop, her mouth firming with a look Sidney knew all too well.

"No big deal," she announced airily. "There's no reason why you can't be the fourth as Miss Lorraine planned."

When Katherine started to object, Megan caught her by the arm and gently propelled her toward the door. "You're worried about leaving when we have a guest." She glanced back at Sidney. "You won't mind, huh, Sid?"

When Sidney shook her head wordlessly, Megan turned for additional support from the group in the pool. "Y'all won't mind if Grammy ducks out early, will you?" she said, clearly expecting no opposition from anyone. She ushered Katherine through the door, adding magnanimously, "Take the Buick, Grammy. No one needs it tonight."

Sidney wouldn't look at Beau who stood beside her in the pool. But she felt the quiver that ran through him and knew that he was enjoying Megan's blithe handling of the situation. In two minutes, she was back with her friends. Nonchalantly, the teenager avoided glancing directly at either her uncle or Sidney.

"Okay, gang!" she sang out, jumping back into the pool. "How about some volleyball!"

Thoughtfully, but with amusement brimming in her eyes, Sidney turned to Beau. "Do you get the idea that we're all pawns in a master plan?"

Beau shrugged helplessly, his eyes dancing.

"I just hope the plot is finished for the evening," she muttered, then laughed as the orange ball streaked across the pool directly into her hands. She was searching wildly for a receiver when a teenage boy appeared from the garage area. She hadn't spent the past few months in Megan's confidence without recognizing Chip Craddock, a blond brawny sixteen-year-old who had figured significantly in Megan's fantasies for weeks. With a fatalistic resignation, Sidney watched him saunter up. Megan hauled herself out of the pool with a self-possession that Sidney had to admire, considering that the girl confided to her not a week ago that she would trade her Sony Walkman for a date with Chip Craddock.

"The plot thickens," Beau drawled in her ear, watching Megan and Chip talk. The girl squealed over something Chip said and turned eagerly to relay the news to Stacey and Melanie. The two girls quickly got out of the pool and skipped toward the cabana where Sidney knew their clothes were. Megan approached Sidney and Beau with a casual air.

"Guess what Chip got for his birthday," she said, dividing a bright look between both of them.

"A new car," Sidney said instantly, earning surprised looks from Megan and Beau.

"How did you know?"

"His father financed it through the Peabody and I happened to see the paperwork."

"Oh." Megan seemed nonplussed, but only for a second. "Would you be offended if Stacey, Melanie and I went for a ride in it, Sidney?" Her look was laced with just the right touch of wistfulness and apology. And seeing Sidney's exasperation, she plunged on in a hurried whisper, "I know this is *so* rude, Sid, but you know better than anyone how much I wanted Chip to ask me out. Not that this is exactly a date," she said with disarming candor, "but it's the closest thing he's come to it yet." She threw a quick look over her shoulder where her cohorts waited expectantly.

"Go, Megan," Sidney said evenly.

Megan beamed a smile and hugged Sidney. "Thanks, Sid," she whispered. "I'll see you later. Y'all have fun!"

A heavy silence stretched between Beau and Sidney as they watched Megan and her friends disappear into the dusk-darkened evening.

What now? Sidney's thoughts tumbled over one another, mixed with a heightening awareness of the man, big and quiet, beside her. The very thing she'd wanted to avoid had happened. She was alone with him.

Nerves robbed her of the rest of her composure. "That was the most blatantly shameless stunt Megan has ever tried," she sputtered, groping through the water toward the steps.

"Yeah, thank God she's in the family," Beau murmured wryly. "I can use management talent like that."

She turned to him fiercely. "Why didn't you stop her? You know she planned the whole thing! She didn't forget to give Katherine any message. And she knew Chip was coming. This was a silly juvenile caper designed to throw us together, and you let her get away with it!"

Her foot found the first step and she hauled herself out of the pool with Beau right behind her. As she grabbed a large towel and started to dry her soaked hair, Beau caught her arm.

"Was it really that awful, Sidney?" he demanded softly, tugging her around and placing his other hand on her arm.

She had the towel clutched in both fists, pressed against her chest. "You shouldn't encourage her in this," she choked, not looking at him.

"I didn't encourage her," he said simply, his thumbs beginning a hypnotic stroking on her skin. "I just didn't discourage her."

She tossed the towel aside. "You certainly didn't!" She looked up at him and her indignation died as she encountered the expression lurking in his golden eyes.

"Would a man resist a taste of heaven if it was offered?"

Oh, Lord. She was suddenly acutely conscious that too much of her flesh was exposed to his hungry gaze.

Too late she regretted throwing down the towel. Her hands fluttered up to try to cover herself, but he caught them, locking her wrists at her sides.

"You are so beautiful," he breathed, his eyes urgently roaming over her, from the swell of her breasts down and over to the flare of her hips. When he brought his gaze back to hers, her heart turned over.

"I'm glad they're gone. I wanted to be alone with you." He released her wrists and spanned her waist with his hands. Weakly, her eyes closed and she began to tremble.

"And if it took Megan's outrageous plan to arrange it, so be it."

Every conscious thought flew out of her head as his lips caught hers and treated her to a sweetly devastating kiss. With a sigh, she yielded to the inevitable, stepping into his arms as naturally as breathing. Masterfully, he gathered her close, one hand on her spine, the other splayed widely at the small of her back, molding her against the strong thrust of his hips.

Sidney caught his shoulders and let her fingers delight in the muscles that rippled beneath his smooth skin. He was so utterly male, she thought, luxuriating in the feel of him, responding to his touch with all the sweetness of awakened passion.

A deep growl rumbled in his chest as his tongue overcame the barrier of her teeth and swept inside, intent on possession. She whimpered in response to the rough skirmish of his tongue against hers, as he explored every nuance of her mouth, tasting and nipping, making no effort to curb his desire. Enthralled, Sidney made a small cry, wanting more and more, as a strange need kindled inside.

Tenderly, he placed her on a lounge and came down beside her, anchoring her with the weight of his thigh. "I've wanted you like this for so long," he groaned, capturing her welcome cry with his hungry mouth. He slid his palm along the sleek line of her rib cage and waist, then up to cup her breast. He took his mouth from hers and pulled back. One hand went to the tie that held the bikini top. His gaze caught and held hers.

"Do you want this, Sidney?"

The eyes that gazed into his were love-softened, heavy-lashed. She couldn't speak. His thumb raked an aroused nipple and sent a fierce pleasure streaking through her.

"Beau..."

"Tell me you want this, Sidney."

Both thumbs worked hypnotically back and forth, sending her spinning out beyond the stars. His dark golden eyes burned into hers.

"Ah, Beau. Please."

With a deep sigh of satisfaction, he tossed the top aside and bent his head. His mouth just touched the soft swell of her breasts. She shivered as his warm breath caressed her skin, moaning softly as his tongue explored the fragrant cleft and then gently raked her flesh with his teeth.

She tossed her head restlessly, arching and straining to capture all of the pleasure promised by his mouth and hands.

"Oh, sweetheart, didn't I tell you?" he demanded with rough passion.

"What?" She could barely move her lips to speak. All of her bones were melting.

"Didn't I tell you how good we were together?"

Gently, he tugged at one nipple with his teeth, and as she held her breath, he took her fully into the wet warm cavern of his mouth. Instantly, she was flung into new and uncharted territory. She felt lost in pleasure, swamped by sensations that until this moment she'd never dreamed existed.

Sidney could summon none of the restraint that had always been second nature to her. Instead, she turned more fully into his embrace, blindly catching his head and pressing it against her. She was both thrilled and fearful when she felt him, powerful and urgent, against her. Instinctively, she arched into his surging masculinity.

"Sidney," Beau gasped, tearing his mouth from her. "Let me take you inside. I don't want our first time to be on a lounge beside the pool. Anybody could walk up."

He pushed away, catching her hand to pull her toward the patio doors on legs that threatened to buckle any second.

"Wait." Sidney swayed and put a hand out as though to anchor a world that was tilting crazily. She felt Beau's quick look and heard the rough uneven cadence of his breathing. Her gaze went to, then skittered off, the blatant evidence of his arousal before she closed her eyes in a desperate bid to compose herself. "Please wait."

"What is it, Sidney?" Beau caught her chin, forcing her eyes to his. "Are you saying wait and we'll go to your place, or wait while you think of some way to refuse what we both want?"

"I don't want this!"

"You wanted it pretty bad two minutes ago!"

Desperately, she looked around for the wretched bikini top. *What was she thinking of!* One more minute and she would have . . .

"Here." Beau held out the towel.

"Thank you," she whispered, quickly and thankfully wrapping it around her shoulders and clutching it tightly against her breasts. Even in her humiliated state, the rough texture of the towel was both pain and pleasure.

"I think it's time for me to go home," she told him, forcing herself to meet the anger and thwarted desire she knew lurked in his eyes. Yes, it was there, but he was also puzzled and confused.

"I do have the right to say no, don't I?" she challenged with as much dignity as she could muster.

She faced him like an adversary, her composure a frail thing. She didn't know what he thought and she told herself she didn't care. She couldn't get involved with Beau. *She couldn't!* There were too many unknowns between them to recklessly succumb to the desire that raged in them both. But how was she going to keep from it? a tiny voice inside taunted. Everything about him was so like the ideal man she'd always dreamed of—the man she had saved herself for. Next time, she worried, next time would she be able to call a halt before it was too late?

The ride home was silent. Sidney was subdued. She didn't know quite what to expect from Beau. She'd had considerable experience trying to placate frustrated males in her time. Once she'd refused their advances, most of them managed to get in a cheap shot or two. She'd learned to accept that with a philosophical shrug of her shoulders.

But Beau didn't take any cheap shots, nor did he show by word or deed that he was angry with her. He was thoughtfully quiet as he drove through the night streets. And when they walked to her door, he calmly unlocked it before casually taking her tote bag from her and tossing it inside.

Then wordlessly, he caught her close, kissing her with a fierceness that plunged all her senses into chaos again. She swayed a little when he released her and gently urged her inside. Then he was gone, leaving her eyes full of dreams.

Chapter Nine

What you're asking will take time, Ms. James, a lot of time." An obstinate look pursed Oliver Petrie's thin mouth, giving Sidney a glimpse of the dislike she'd always sensed from him. "I'm afraid I can't allow my staff to put aside their regular duties without clearance from Mr. Rutledge."

How would it look, Sidney mused wryly, if she just calmly jerked Petrie's glasses off his face and hit him with them? She sighed and resisted the urge. She needed cooperation, not a confrontation. Petrie was one of those people who would not tolerate intrusion into his professional domain. Ruefully, she supposed it must seem to him that all she wanted to do lately was poke and pry into the accounting records. And it was possible that he might be a tiny bit justified, she admitted reluctantly.

She wanted more complete access to historical data. She swallowed the blunt retort she would've liked to deliver to the pompous little tyrant and forced a smile. "I won't need your staff to help me pull this information, Mr. Petrie, so that problem doesn't apply," she reasoned. "All I need is access to records without having to approach one of your people for every single item. Surely you agree that this is the sensible way to get the job done."

Petrie's eyes flicked to hers. "That may be, Ms. James, assuming this job is authorized. In any case, Mr. Rutledge is still the only one who can give you unlimited access to my records."

Back in her office, Sidney fumed, wishing harder than ever that she could vent her frustration with violence. It had been useless to waste time trying to wheedle Petrie around. One look at his face and she'd known it was hopeless. He was suspicious of her insistent efforts to scrutinize the records. But the feeling was mutual. Sidney was becoming suspicious of Petrie's determined tactics to obstruct her.

Thoughtfully, she turned her attention to the papers in front of her and the random collection of data she'd compiled over the past week. She tapped a pencil idly. This morning she'd arrived early, burning with determination to match up all the random data and discover, once and for all, what was going on here. If she could do that, she knew she'd solve the riddle of Beau Rutledge.

Beau. Inevitably her thoughts turned to him. And inevitably she was seized with an urgent need to resolve all her doubts about him. Then she would be free to...to what? She sank into her chair.

Her whole body flushed when she remembered how close she'd come last night to surrendering to the fiery passion he'd kindled between them. The whole evening had been a slow seduction. From the moment he'd picked her up—no, from the moment he'd called her that morning, she'd been subjected to a sweetly compelling seduction. Her head recognized the danger, but her heart had a will of its own. Her head urged caution because of the scraps of Memphis gossip and Atlanta scandal, but her heart recognized something deep and compelling that would not be crushed. But oh, when he'd revealed the details of his marriage and Lisa's betrayal, she'd wanted nothing so much as to put her arms around him, to console him with her lips and hands and body. Even inexperienced as she was, he evoked the deepest feminine response from her.

She had been so wrong about Beau. He wasn't an unprincipled libertine. In fact, the events of the weekend had revealed him as a caring, tender and indulgent man. She pressed urgent fingers to her lips. What would he say when he discovered that she'd handed Lisa the weapons to destroy his marriage and probably his business?

"Good morning." Startled, she lifted her eyes and collided with Beau's warm gaze. He looked wonderful. Propped against the door in jeans, he was tall and long legged, his white polo shirt open, his sun-streaked hair wind tossed. He smelled like sunshine and after-shave and was all male.

When she only stared, one tawny brow arched cockily. "Overachieving again?"

She collected her wits and smiled, glancing at her watch. "It's ten-thirty. Does that make you underachieving?"

His answering grin was slightly off center. "How'd you like an aerial look at the number three mill?"

She looked blank. "You mean from an airplane?"

"You know of any other way to get an aerial?" He pushed away from the doorframe and came over to her. With easy familiarity, he rested one hip on her desk and leafed through her papers. "Have you got any figures on operational capacity of number three?"

Forcing aside the leaping response of her pulse, she concentrated on the question. "Yes. It's the weakest link in your program."

His glance was quick and puzzled. "Program?"

She gave a half laugh. "My terminology for the systematic goals that must be met for you to achieve a profit that will keep Rutledge Enterprises solvent."

He looked impressed, and she saw with a little rush of pleasure that there was no mockery in his expression.

"Okay, is number three operating at seventy-five percent capacity?"

A tiny line formed between her brows. "That's what you need from number three, but I show it to be less than forty percent."

He grinned and straightened. "Bingo! As promised, the Peabody's ace accountant has a handle on the situation. So, why don't we take a quick trip down there and see what's holding up production."

She saw that he expected her to drop everything and get right up and go with him. And Sidney discovered that she would like nothing better than to go with him— anywhere. She banked down half a dozen reasons why she shouldn't, telling herself it was an opportunity to delve into the company's secrets that she couldn't afford to pass by. But whatever the reason, she was going to fall in with his plan.

"This is official business?" she wanted to know. It was one thing to admit her weakness for him to herself, but another entirely to let him know it.

"Yes ma'am," he drawled. "You just watch those guys at number three snap to it when they realize they're being inspected by the Peabody's best."

She threw him a suspicious look, expecting sarcasm, but encountering only an incredible blend of tenderness and stark desire.

She found herself standing, allowing herself to be nudged toward the door. Putty in his hands, she told herself wryly.

"But why do you need me to come?" she asked, a little breathless for some reason. "The reports come in to Petrie each month." They were headed for the Blazer.

"Uh-huh."

She tried to interpret that, but his expression revealed nothing.

"I want to take a look at the physical operation, and you can take a look at the books," he informed her, pulling out of the parking lot and accelerating with typical male aggressiveness.

Did he have his own suspicions? Sidney wondered, slanting a look at him as he drove. "You have the figures," she pointed out. "Everything's in the computer."

He shrugged, preoccupied with the traffic. "Maybe," he stated laconically. "Maybe not."

He *was* suspicious! Sidney settled back while her thoughts leaped ahead. Beau obviously had some motive for a personal visit to the mill. And for taking her along. From under the fringe of her lashes, she studied him. He wouldn't just invite her for the pleasure of her company. Would he? She turned her gaze straight ahead, her thoughts churning. She blinked, surprised. She'd just noticed they weren't headed for the airport. They were within two blocks of her apartment.

"I thought you might want to change into jeans or something a little less...feminine. Number three is pretty remote and the facilities tend to be a bit informal."

"Do the men stay overnight?" she asked curiously.

"Some do, some don't. If they live within a reasonable distance, they may stay during the week and go home for weekends. Bed and board is there, if they choose. Living like they do, the men are pretty laid-back." His golden eyes swept over her butterscotch shirtwaist dress and ivory heels. "Not that you won't command instant attention in that outfit."

"You're going to command instant attention in those jeans too," Beau commented forty-five minutes later as they made their way across the runway of the airport toward a blue and white Cessna.

She shot him a suspicious look. "Are you sure this is official business?"

"Trust me," he said, his voice low and deep.

Sidney's stomach dropped as the Cessna lifted skyward. There was no point in trying to convince herself that the sensation was anything except the inevitable reaction she got whenever she was close to Beau. She glanced over at him and found him watching her, a corner of his mouth tilted in a smile. What stole her breath away was the look in his eyes.

The Cessna was noisy, making conversation almost impossible. The pilot, Jace Winslow, pointed out a few landmarks but mostly the flight was silent. Sidney was relieved. She was simply not ready to deal with the passion and tenderness that lurked in the golden depths of Beau's eyes whenever he looked at her.

"Are we close?" she questioned when they seemed to be reducing air speed. She looked out, seeing nothing but an undulating green carpet that stretched endlessly.

Beau pointed over the left wing to a fire tower. "That's about the center point of number three tract," he said.

Sidney glanced at her watch. They'd covered the nearly seventy miles to the site in a remarkably short time. The Cessna was reducing altitude when Beau suddenly tensed and signaled the pilot to bank steeply. As they made another pass, he leaned over and touched Jace's shoulder, indicating a thin wisp of smoke curling out of the dense growth on the western edge of Rutledge land.

Beau smothered an oath. "Fire!" He quickly stripped off his seatbelt and turned in his seat, straining to see. Jace reached into a side compartment and withdrew a pair of binoculars. Silently, he passed them to Beau.

"Jace, radio number three and alert them," Beau ordered. His mouth was grim as he studied the horizon to try to pinpoint the fire, listening with set features as Jace relayed the information.

The response from the Cessna's radio sounded garbled to Sidney, but apparently Beau was satisfied. He refastened his seatbelt. "Set this thing down as quick as you can, Jace."

The pilot nodded. "Two minutes and you'll be fightin' fire, buddy!"

Sidney paled as she realized what he meant. Surely Beau wouldn't actually get close to the fire! Out of control, a forest fire was a threat to people as well as animals and property.

The landing strip was a short stretch of blacktop a couple of hundred yards from the field office. The instant the Cessna touched down, Beau was tearing at his seatbelt. Men and vehicles were being readied to head for the fire site, but as Beau jumped from the Cessna, one truck veered out toward the landing strip.

Sidney scrambled out, poised to jump the short distance off the wing, but Beau caught her waist, setting her on her feet. "I'm sorry about this, baby," he said, throwing a quick glance at the truck that bounced and jolted across the field toward them. His hands idly explored her rib cage. "I don't have to tell you what a disaster a fire can be, especially in July when conditions are this dry. You stay in the field office and don't leave, no matter what," he told her sternly.

An awful feeling seared Sidney's chest. She threw an anxious glance toward the rapidly approaching truck. She could see two men inside, hear the fire-fighting gear clattering where it had been tossed into the back of the pickup.

"Beau, you're not going with them, are you?"

His hands at her waist tightened as he watched the tense play of emotions on her face. "I have to, sweetheart. I'm the only one who knows exactly where the fire is. I might be able to save time. I hope to God we can douse it quickly."

The truck was almost upon them and Sidney's apprehension grew. "But they've all been trained for this and you haven't," she pleaded, anxiety robbing her of all pretense. It seemed the most natural thing in the world to show the man she loved that she was fearful for him.

Beau wrapped a hand around her nape and brought her mouth to his. His kiss was hard and promising. And too brief. She kissed him back wildly, more in stress and fear than passion.

He caught her hands from around his neck and gently brought them to his chest where he squeezed them reassuringly. "That, for your information, Sidney James, wasn't official business," he breathed roughly, his voice uneven. The truck drew up in a cloud of dust and he turned to go.

"Be careful," she murmured, her green eyes saying a thousand other things.

He grinned and climbed in beside a burly-looking lumberjack. "Hold that thought."

Sidney walked into the field office dazed by more than the outbreak of a forest fire. *She had fallen in love with Beau Rutledge!* In spite of all her determination to steer clear of him, in spite of the unflattering things she'd believed about him, she'd lost her heart to him. She drifted over to one dusty window and gazed out over Rutledge land, admitting at last that she had been more than halfway in love with him from the beginning. Possibly even from the time she'd had him under her surveillance at the Thompson Agency.

On that thought she groaned, abandoning the window and flopping down onto a hard oversize executive chair. What was Beau going to say when he discovered her connection with Thompson's? What was he going to do? Her fingers worried at a ball-point pen on the desk. He was attracted to her, Sidney knew. He wanted her. But already, she'd seen how effectively he'd controlled his physical desire when he'd judged her unsuitable. In spite of his initial attraction, he'd easily resisted her.

She jumped up, agitated and anxious, blocking out images of Beau burned and hurt, who knows how far out in a desolate tract of land with no medical facility for miles. She looked down and saw her hands trembling. *This would never do!* She would have to find something to occupy herself. What would Beau think when he came back to find her acting like a spineless ninny?

Grimly, she surveyed the sawmill office. Every man had responded to the threat of fire. She was totally alone. Calming gradually, she looked around curiously. What had been Beau's reason for coming here today? He wanted to check what was holding up production and she was to take a look at the books.

She moved purposefully toward the only progressive-looking piece of office equipment. Sure enough, it was a compatible unit to her IBM. She felt a tiny thrill. At last, she had total access! She grabbed her own printouts and, pushing Beau and danger to the back of her mind, she sat down and began searching.

Two hours of concentration produced some very interesting information. She was hardly surprised to discover major discrepancies between the numbers at the mill and the reports transmitted to the main office. Her mouth had a grim look as the importance of her discovery dawned. In very little time, the shortages would become acute. That circumstance would have a domino effect. First would come a partial shutdown of the main plant, making it impossible to maintain the vital seventy-five percent production rate. Then, when that was a reality, the stock options would fall to Vince Trehern.

Vince Trehern. Sidney's eyes became thoughtful and her brain raced. He'd made a couple of visits to the main plant while she'd been there and he'd also seemed friendly with Oliver Petrie. In fact, on thinking back, Petrie was far more welcoming to Vince Trehern than Trehern's business warranted. Whatever his business was.

Was it possible? Had she stumbled on the explanation for the discrepancies, the puzzling inconsistencies that she'd uncovered in her financial sleuthing? She sucked in an excited breath. It was. She had. She felt it in her bones.

She went back with renewed determination to search out as much information as she could. This was what Louis had suspected and she wanted to present him with professionally documented evidence. As for Beau, she decided not to mention anything just yet. He had enough pressure and stress just managing the shaky Rutledge interests.

Besides, why deny it? She wanted to satisfy herself that Beau wasn't involved. There still remained the question of exactly who was responsible. Everything in her denied that Beau would be the most logical individual. She wouldn't believe it and she needed a little time to ferret out the person who was.

She was pouring herself a cup of coffee when she heard the first truck approaching. She put the mug down, her heart lodged in her throat, and ran to the door. Two trucks drew up and four or five men piled out. Sidney had eyes for only one. He was dirty, smoke darkened and grinning. He'd never looked better to her hungry eyes.

He took the stairs in one leap and caught her up, lifting her over his head and turning her around in a jubilant hug.

"Beau!" She threw a quick look at the curious grinning crew.

"We doused it, sugar!" His golden eyes danced with triumph and sheer male exuberance. He eased her down, every inch of her plastered against him, heedless of his grimy clothes and her clean ones. "Did you miss me?"

She forgot the crew and buried her nose in the tawny tuft at the top of his shirt as she'd always longed to.

Beau chuckled and caught two handfuls of her hair, guiding her mouth to his. His lips swooped down and claimed her in a quick kiss. Then, holding her hand, he led her back into the office.

"Oh Beau," she whispered. "I ... Are you okay?"

"I've never been more okay," he assured her, hugging her and sweeping an audacious tongue in her ear, then nipping the tender lobe with a growl.

She sagged against him, and he laughed, giving her a final loud smacking kiss on her lips, and leaned back to survey his handiwork.

"What?" she said shakily when he just stared with those fantastic topaz eyes.

"I'm just complimenting myself on the best idea I've had in a long time."

"What idea?"

"Hustling you down here to number three."

Her mouth opened indignantly. "Official business, you said!" she retorted without heat.

He chuckled. "Is this your idea of official business?" He moved suggestively, his thighs touching her softness. Her eyes darkened to a storm-green. His closeness and the newly discovered state of her emotions had her leaning pliantly into him.

"Very professional," he mocked.

She felt color rise in her cheeks. "It's still not too late to do some work," she threatened.

His fingers moved affectionately along her jaw. "Always the conscientious little Peabody person," he teased.

"You brought me here to look over the books," she reminded him primly, "and that's what I did." But a part of her was ridiculously pleased that he hadn't sounded resentful about her connection to the Peabody.

Beau glanced out the window where dusk was quickly falling. "Which reminds me, I haven't had a chance to check out the production problems. Jace had another commitment and was to pick us up around four for the flight back to Memphis. I had to use the shortwave on the truck to let him know I couldn't leave as we'd planned."

She stared into his eyes, marveling at the thick tangle of male lashes. Entirely too long and lush for a man, she thought with blatant prejudice. He was exhausted. With the eyes of love, she saw the fatigue that blunted his features.

"Sidney," he prompted, tugging gently on her hair. "We can drive thirty minutes or so and try to find a decent motel, or we can stay here overnight in the crew's quarters. It's up to you."

"I don't mind staying here," she told Beau, warming at the look in his eyes. "I did some exploring today and checked out the crew's quarters."

He tilted his tawny head. "You're sure?"

"I'm sure."

It was no big deal. The quarters were separated into two units, each with six bunks. At least she would have some privacy. And, to her surprise, there were two bathrooms, each with a couple of man-size shower stalls.

The rest of the afternoon flew by, and in no time dusk had turned to pitch-black night. Some of the crew left, tired and dragging, while half a dozen men stayed. After Beau showered, he took Sidney into the dining room and together they shared a meal that could not be faulted by anyone's standards.

"You're tired," she said later as he sprawled in the executive chair studying the daily reports submitted by Jim Mason, number three manager. She ran her eyes over his rumpled form, dressed in a blue chambray work shirt that was a little snug across the shoulders. His sun-kissed hair was in disarray from his fingers raking through it as he'd struggled frustratedly with Mason's reports.

"I can't get a fix on this tonight," he said finally, tossing the papers aside in disgust. "I've got to wait for Jim tomorrow."

For a moment, silence stretched between them. Then Beau shot her a straight look. "Do you think I can pull it out, Sidney?"

She sat a little straighter, startled. Did he want his ego stroked or was he asking because he valued her professional opinion?

"It's very important to you to turn Rutledge Enterprises around, isn't it?" she asked.

"I'm going to turn it around," he stated flatly. "I just wondered what you thought my chances are."

"You can do it," she said, wondering if she should mention the endangered shares. But how could she if she didn't follow it up with her discoveries this afternoon on the computer? Not yet. "Just keep a close watch on the output of this mill and the most serious threat is eliminated.''

He nodded. Then, frowning, ''I'm still trying to work out how Ben got in trouble so quickly. Putting shares in jeopardy, neglecting maintenance on equipment.'' He shook his head, bewildered. ''Some of Ben's reckless decisions were made while my father was still alive. I can't understand why the old man didn't object.''

''Maybe he did and Ben wouldn't listen.''

''No way. When my old man spoke, everyone listened.''

''When you were young, maybe. But he'd already lost one son with his rigid attitude. Perhaps he feared losing the other.''

He studied her. ''Apparently you know the story,'' he said with a cynical bite in his voice. ''Headstrong number two son, the hell-raiser, irresponsible devil cub that not even John Rutledge was able to curb.''

''Too much like John Rutledge himself?'' she offered with a soft smile.

''I'm going to save his company,'' he stated grimly.

''Yes,'' she agreed softly, her heart melting at the fierce satisfaction he took in her words.

''Beau, would you speak to Oliver Petrie and authorize my access to the full computer setup?''

He frowned thoughtfully. ''Did you find something today?''

She hesitated. ''I'm not sure. Maybe. If I could search thoroughly, I could answer that. It could be nothing.''

''Okay, I'll tell Petrie.''

''Thanks.''

Suddenly he stood, stretching his arms high above his head, exposing a band of tanned flesh at his taut waist.

Even in the too-small blue chambray, he was sexy, his all-male appeal heightened by his sleepy rumpled appearance.

He looked at her. "Is it too early to hit the sack?"

She jumped up. "Of course not," she said too quickly, banishing wicked delicious thoughts of her hand stroking his flat stomach, tangling in the tawny hair that bisected it.

"Did you have enough privacy to take a shower?" he asked, splaying one large hand widely on the small of her back and urging her down the hall toward the sleeping quarters. At the door, she stepped inside and Beau quickly followed, turning her and burying his face in her russet hair. "Mmm, I can tell you did. Your hair smells like spice."

"It was the only shampoo they had."

"I'm not complaining." He kicked the door shut with his foot. "You always smell wonderful." He nipped at her lobe. "You taste wonderful." A hand slid beneath her shirt and captured a breast. "You *feel*—"

"Beau . . ." Her control was slipping fast.

His lips skimmed over her face, searching for her mouth. "Am I repeating myself?"

"You've got to stop this, Beau," she moaned, trying not to drown in a sea of sensuality.

"Why are we always in the wrong place when it's time to make love?" he anguished, his busy mouth seeking out the underside of her jaw.

She laughed shakily, relieved not to have to refuse him again tonight. But time was running out. Soon there would be a right time and a right place. And before that time she would have to tell him the part she'd played at the Thompson Agency. Until then, oh, how she wanted to lose herself in the magic of him.

He gave her a last reluctant kiss and grinned. "Which do you want, the window side or the wall side? I don't think you're the top bunk type."

"What?"

His tawny brows lifted. "You *are* the top bunk type?"

"What are you talking about?" She laughed, looking bewildered.

"To sleep, sweetheart. Where do you want to sleep?"

Warily, she stared at him. "Surely you don't mean that you're going to sleep in here with me?"

The look he gave her was slow, assessing. "Did you see those six men at supper tonight?" he asked mildly.

Silence was her only answer.

"You said you toured the crew's quarters. There are six bunks on each side and six men. Not counting me."

She backed away then, coming up against the edge of a bunk. "You know I assumed you were sleeping with the crew," she replied, an accusing note entering her voice.

"I asked you if you wanted to drive to a motel and you said no."

"I'm driving to one now," she said decisively, looking around for her purse.

"No, you're not!" He caught her arm and whipped her around. "It's one-thirty in the morning, Sidney. Stop acting like a scared virgin. You've said no and I accept that. There's no reason why we can't share this room!" He threw a look around the rustic surroundings. "It's at least thirty feet long and half that wide."

Sidney chewed her lip and grudgingly admitted that he was right.

"I don't suppose you would even consider shedding those tight jeans and using a man's T-shirt to sleep in," he said with chilling sarcasm. "We have plenty."

She felt grungy and uncomfortable even though she'd taken a shower earlier. Longingly, she thought of the soft comfort of a T-shirt, but...

"Here." He tossed it to her and pushed her, none too gently, toward the bathroom. "I'll give you five minutes and then I'm getting in that bunk over there." Without waiting for more arguments, he stomped out.

She quickly shed the jeans and her knit shirt, feeling silly and inexperienced. But darn it, she *was* inexperienced! A bunkhouse with a snoring crew across the hall wasn't how she wanted to be initiated into the joy of sex. She paused, pulling the big T-shirt over her head. It would be joy with Beau, too. She knew that with every female instinct she had. She yanked the T-shirt on. But not until she could come to him openly and honestly.

She walked out of the bathroom with as much dignity as the T-shirt permitted, but it was a wasted effort since her five minutes weren't up and Beau was nowhere around. She slid into the bunk and was pulling a sheet over her when he came back.

He didn't spare a glance in her direction but flipped off the light and then took off his clothes in stony silence.

Crickets and night sounds were loud in the tense stillness in the room. Desperately, Sidney tried to block a vivid fantasy of Beau naked—tan and tawny and virile. It was...

"Why *did* you act like a scared virgin, Sidney?" Beau's voice came out quiet and deep. He sounded hurt.

She waited a long minute. "Maybe because I am," she returned huskily.

He went absolutely still, stunned. For seconds he lay intensely absorbing the incredible wonder of it. She had never given herself completely. To anyone. All that womanly appeal, that fragile beauty, was untouched. It was almost too much to take in.

He raised himself on one elbow to get up and turn on a light.

"Don't," she whispered, stopping him. Then, with stinging honesty, "You don't have to tell me that a twenty-five-year-old virgin is pretty freaky, considering the enlightened times we live in."

"Not to mention precious. And special. And wonderful."

"Thank you."

He heard the smile in her voice.

"You're so beautiful," he murmured, dazed. "How did you hold them all off?"

Her wry chuckle rippled over his heartstrings. "Would you believe it never required much effort? Before."

But Beau was so astonished that he missed that last telltale word. He sank back, marveling over his fantastic luck. Because he intended to have her. Sidney was the woman for him, he'd known it from the first instant he'd seen her. How could he not have guessed? All the signs had been there. Now he understood that endearing hint of shyness and sweet vulnerability, her inexplicable retreat when he'd been close to taking her. All that delicious response she'd shown in his arms. New to her. Oh, how sweet it would be to love her. All night. A fierce elemental craving flooded his bloodstream and he bit off a moan.

A soft slow smile curled his mouth. His topaz eyes were night-dark. Her days were numbered. Oh yeah, her days were numbered.

Chapter Ten

Have you developed schizophrenia?"

Sidney's laugh came out in a rush as she pedaled the exercise bicycle. "Are you suggesting I'm a bit moody lately?"

Jill's eyes rolled heavenward. "A bit! Look, we're talking euphoria or the dregs of depression here, my friend. One day sunshine, the next day rain. Now come on, give. Tell mother."

Sidney sighed, shaking her head. "I guess I couldn't suggest that you mind your own business."

"Well, you can suggest it, but considering how many tears I cried on your shoulder over Mike, I'm not likely to do it."

"Rutledge Enterprises has turned out to be a very demanding assignment, Jill."

"The job is demanding, or Beau Rutledge is demanding?" said the shrewd and canny Jill.

"Well..."

"Just what is he demanding?"

"Unconditional surrender."

The bell went on the exercise bicycle and Sidney quit thankfully. She climbed off and sank to the floor like a doll with the stuffing removed. Jill dropped down beside her and crossed her legs in a lotus position.

"So what's the problem?" she wanted to know, eyeing Sidney's strained features. "And don't try to tell me you're not in love with Beau Rutledge, Sid, because I know you too well. At last you've fallen, and I don't know who's luckier. He's a prince of a guy and so are you."

"I've always wanted to be a princess," Sidney murmured with a faint stab at humor.

"You know what I mean, Sid."

Sidney sighed unhappily. "You know that job I had with the Thompson Agency that you thought was so glamorous and sensational?" She flicked a questioning look at Jill who nodded. "Well, one of our clients was Lisa Rutledge."

Jill frowned. "So you'd met him before?"

"Not exactly."

"Well, then what exactly?"

"I was assigned to her case. I was the one who provided Lisa Rutledge with the information that she used to divorce Beau and blacken his name in Atlanta."

"Oh, no, Sid." Jill reached out and touched Sidney's arm sympathetically.

"I'm not sure, but I think she got an unfair portion of the communal property, too. You know, the business and their home."

"What did he say when you told him?"

Sidney's eyes stung as she fought the urge to cry. "That's just it, Jilly. I haven't told him." She rushed on when Jill's mouth opened imperiously. "I know I'm going to have to and I will."

"When?"

"Soon."

"Well, one thing," Jill offered bracingly, "he's a reasonable man; he'll probably be upset at first, but he knows you now. When you explain that it was your job and nothing personal, I'm sure he'll understand."

"Come on, Jill. He's going to despise me and you know it. In fact, he's already called me a sleazy detective, not knowing it was me he was talking about."

"I think I followed that garbled statement," Jill said dryly.

"And if that isn't enough, I've been collecting data from the company's records that could reverse all the progress Beau has made since he's been in charge."

"Oh, Sidney!"

"So, what do you think?" Sidney said tiredly. "Is that reason enough to be moody?" She got slowly to her feet, her dancer's body uncurling gracefully. "I need to get back to the office. I probably shouldn't have left in the middle of the day, but Beau had that look in his eye, and I'm almost out of excuses to avoid him."

"You've got to tell him, Sid."

Sidney waved a hand and disappeared into the shower room.

Her little office was beginning to feel like a prison to Sidney. She dropped her purse negligently onto a chair and started right back where she'd left off before going to Jill's Place. Fortunately Beau had been good as his word. He'd personally ordered that she be allowed access to the whole accounting system even though Petrie had strenuously objected. Sidney had her own ideas as to why the man was so upset. She suspected the accountant's main objection had been the unexpectedness of Beau's order. And if that were so, Sidney was very interested in finding out why. Would Petrie have done some skillful cover-up if he'd had any warning that Sidney was suddenly going to see everything? Time and some serious investigation would tell, Sidney thought to herself as she settled down to the task.

Two hours later, she decided that Petrie would indeed have benefited from a warning. Here in front of her was the evidence that she'd been searching for. Reports from number three were being changed to show less mill work than was actually accomplished. Then the shortages were being reported to the main office while the actual production differences and the illicit profits were being raked off into the hands of . . . who?

Sidney's fingers actually trembled with excitement. It would be interesting to see Petrie's bank account records for the past year as well as Vince Trehern's. They had to be in on this together. Unless—

No! She banished that thought before it was fully formed. There was no way that Beau could be a part of anything so corrupt. Besides, why would he? Could he be raking in huge sums of money knowing the company was doomed? Sidney stared hard at the window, her eyes going to Beau's Blazer. She recalled that first day, his resentment of her. But now that she knew about Lisa, she believed his feelings stemmed from past hurts, not from a need to keep an accountant from getting into the records of his company. No, it was not Beau who was pillaging the company. He had too much integrity, too much honor. And she was ready to stake everything on it—her job, her professional judgment, her heart. Especially her heart.

For the tenth time, she looked at the recap sheet spread out over her desk. If it was sent to Louis Maynard in its current state, it would precipitate a crisis in which the bank and other Rutledge creditors would call in their loans. Surely there was . . .

Her intercom buzzed and she answered curtly.

"Who?" she asked Gail, distracted by the grim numbers in front of her.

"Spencer Foley!" Oh, no! Of all the salesmen in the sunbelt, Spencer Foley was the last one she wanted to see today of all days.

"Sidney, it's great to see you!" Spencer strode into her office, caught both of her hands over her desk and tugged her up for a warm kiss on her cheek.

"Spencer," she murmured politely, sinking back out of reach. "This is a surprise."

"For me, too," he replied promptly. "Imagine the coincidence—my favorite lady right here at Rutledge."

"I wasn't aware that Rutledge Enterprises was one of your clients," she responded faintly, her smile brittle.

"It wasn't until I was promoted. I'm marketing vice-president at Fielding and Koch now," he told her proudly. "Rutledge, of course, is one of the major clients in my new territory, and I wanted to personally visit every one." His blue eyes flicked over her admiringly. "It's an added bonus to find you here, Sidney."

Please, please don't let Beau come in now, Sidney begged capricious fate. If he did, and Spencer happened to mention her job in Atlanta, it would be awful. It was going to be bad enough when she told him at the right time and in the right place. That way, they'd have a chance to work out the problems, especially now that they were both coming to terms with their attraction to each other. After last night surely they could reach an understanding?

"What?" She looked at Spencer blankly, having missed who knows how much of what he'd just said.

"Why are you here? What about your job at the Peabody Bank, Sidney?" He looked disapproving. "You haven't gotten into something unsuitable again, have you?"

"I'm an accountant with the Peabody, Spencer," she told him through clenched teeth. "This is an official assignment."

How could I have ever given this . . . this pompous clown the time of day? she demanded of herself, setting her jaw and about to show him the door.

"I can't imagine Sidney into anything unsuitable," Beau said quietly, entering with a soft tread and a menacing look at Spencer. The look he shot Sidney was less easily defined. "Fielding and Koch's man, I think Gail said?"

Spencer thrust out an eager hand. "Vice-president, marketing. It's a pleasure, Mr. Rutledge."

Beau nodded once and accepted Foley's hand briefly, obviously without pleasure. "You've seen my marketing manager?" Beau inquired coolly.

"Right." Spencer's gaze turned to Sidney. "But I couldn't leave without speaking to Sidney as soon as I discovered she was here. The last time I phoned her, she didn't mention Rutledge." Spencer gave her a gently chastising look, oblivious to the cold disapproval in Beau's topaz eyes.

"What's this about Sidney being into something unsuitable?" Beau inquired with deceptive mildness.

Spencer's look was possessive and his voice took on an indulgent tone. "Well, it's history now but Sidney and I had some fairly strong words about her work with the Thompson Detective Agency," he explained to a suddenly alert Beau. "Can you believe that? Sidney a private eye?" Spencer looked at her fondly, shaking his head. "She makes a pretty unlikely operative, doesn't she?"

Confused, Beau frowned. "Indeed she does."

"Now, income tax," Spencer said expansively, "she's great at that. You wouldn't believe the miracle she worked with my taxes last year. She—"

"Ah, thanks for stopping in, Spencer," Sidney interrupted hastily, moving around her desk and urging him toward the door.

"Well, naturally I'd stop in, Sidney," Spencer assured her, trailing the words over his shoulder as she ushered him unceremoniously out of her office. "I'll call you next week, love."

"Goodbye, Spencer," she hissed, watching him depart. The man was totally unaware of the bomb he'd just dropped, or the electric reaction he'd unwittingly triggered in the two people now locked in silent regard.

"When did you work for the Thompson Agency?" Beau asked, his frown settling into a kind of puzzled apprehension.

Sidney held his gaze for a fragile moment then walked back to her desk, her legs unsteady, and sat down. "I've been meaning to talk to you about that."

Still confused, his eyes followed her jerky movements, watched the way her glance skittered off things in the room, noticed that she did not look at him.

"Was he talking about the same Thompson Agency that I know about?"

She sighed. "Yes, I—"

He shook his head as though to clear it. "You can't mean that you worked for those...lowlifes." He looked at her with disbelief.

She took a deep breath before meeting his incredulous gaze. "I did, Beau, but—"

He shook his head in denial. "No way. You're an accountant! What does an accountant do for a business that specializes in spying?"

This was much worse than she'd feared. She searched her mind trying to come up with an explanation that wouldn't disgust him too much.

"Spying, of course, but records and documents would be more your speed," he said in an almost conversational tone. Then he hesitated. "And computers."

She just looked at him.

He went absolutely still as comprehension dawned. "When did you work for them, Sidney?" he asked, his look fierce and deadly.

She swallowed. "Give me a chance to explain, Beau."

"When?" he demanded with devastating simplicity.

She sighed. "August, two years ago."

She'd seen Beau angry before. And several times that anger had been directed at her. But she'd never seen anything like the fierce outrage that now blazed in his eyes. Never had they looked so hard and so cold.

"Are you the same Thompson operative," he said the word with stinging contempt, "who compiled the garbage that Lisa used to divorce me?"

"Wait, Beau, it's not like you think," she said, her voice breaking with feeling. He wasn't going to understand, she anguished silently. She'd known all along he wouldn't. Suddenly the enormity of what was at stake almost crushed her.

"What is there to explain? You hid behind trees and corners, spying on me, you dragged my secretary's good name in the mud along with mine...." He stopped, spearing her with a telling look. "You even plundered the secrets of my computer, didn't you!"

"It wasn't like that," Sidney denied desperately.

"Then with your excellent credentials," he sneered, "you insinuated yourself into the Peabody Bank and finagled a position to spy on me here!"

"No!"

"Then what!" he roared, at last unleashing his wrath.

"My job with the Thompson Agency was just that—a job!" she reasoned. "I didn't choose the clients they assigned me. Think a minute! I'm a financial detective, Beau. Surveillance was a very small and distasteful aspect of the job with the agency. So distasteful that I couldn't stand to work there very long."

The look he sent her was frankly skeptical. His eyes narrowed with sudden suspicion. "How many other secrets are you hiding, Sidney? Is there anything else about me that you're withholding—saving for just the right moment?" His tone was low and menacing. "Take my advice if you are—it wouldn't be a good idea."

Sidney stared, unable to find any words.

He paused with his hand on the door and shook his head. "You're really something, you know that? That maidenly innocence you use so fetchingly—I nearly believed it." He laughed humorlessly, rolling his eyes. "Hah!"

She inhaled sharply with pain.

"And since your special expertise is in numbers, you must have been aware of the embezzlement racket that was going on in my Atlanta business," he commented almost casually. "Did you believe me guilty there, too?" He shook his head. "Such a busy little detective."

"No, Lisa decided—"

He nodded, his mouth scornful. "Yeah, Lisa. You two must have had a field day totaling up my transgressions."

"Beau, please let me explain!" she cried.

As if he couldn't tolerate the sight of her another second, he left, closing the door with a sharp snap.

For a minute Sidney sat frozen. Indeed, Beau might well ask what other secrets she was withholding. She stared down at her next report to the bank, the one that would seal the fate of Rutledge Enterprises and possibly wrest from Beau his birthright. Tears welled, then overflowed down her cheeks. She covered her face with her hands.

She'd known he would despise her, hadn't she? She'd known he wouldn't really take a tolerant attitude toward the person who had destroyed his marriage and who knew what else. Who could expect it of him?

She scrounged around in her desk, found some tissues and mopped at her tears. Her eyes fell on the report. Her dream of a future with Beau was pretty much destroyed, but—she blew her nose—she was still a professional and Louis was expecting this report. She sniffed, forcing her mind to function. Maybe she could persuade Louis to agree to an extension. Or should she report her findings to Louis, even half-baked as they were? Maybe the best thing would be to rely on Louis and the resources of the Peabody. She rested her head wearily on an elbow, raking her fingers dejectedly through her red curls.

No, she'd better get the extension without revealing the damaging numbers. Then she could go home and think, try to figure out what to do next. Vaguely she nodded, one decision made. After Beau's bitter rejection, what difference would twelve hours make?

Beau slammed the door to his office and strode to the window. How many times would he be taken in by a conniving woman? First Lisa, now Sidney. But, fool that he was, he'd made it easy for Sidney, believing her different from Lisa. His mouth twisted bitterly.

He groaned and propped a hand on the windowsill, staring outside, seeing nothing. Did Sidney's little mystery games give her some kind of perverted pleasure? Lord! Spying on him! He should have trusted his instincts from the first. The minute he learned she was the Peabody spy, he should have asked Louis to replace her. But he'd been put off by her attention to Megan and his mother. And then by her warm giving relationship with her friend, Jill. Not to mention his own lust for her! He swore roundly.

And now to discover that she'd been the one who— By God, she was lucky he hadn't climbed over that stupid computer of hers and choked her!

He blanked out her attempts to explain. Even if she didn't choose the Rutledge assignment, the bottom line was the same, wasn't it? So she couldn't stomach it and quit. So what? He picked up a paper clip and mutilated it, then flicked it across the room in disgust.

Why hadn't she told him? He balled his fist, not allowing himself to release the tension that screamed in him. She should have told him the first day. But had he encouraged any personal revelations between them for the first week, let alone the first day? a bleak voice argued somewhere in the back of his mind.

Then at Megan's party, when he was baring his soul to her—he winced—she could have said something then. She had almost said something. He frowned, trying to recall. He hadn't let her finish, he'd been so eager to explain Lisa and his divorce. That night was the first time they'd ever spent more than a few minutes together without ending at each other's throats. He felt a slight lessening of tension remembering just where they'd ended up that night. Her body, at first wet and cool from the pool, then flushed and heated from his caresses, had been delicious.

He stared morosely into space, seeing her anxious face as she'd begged him not to go to the scene of the fire. Why had she been so anxious? And then, when he'd come back, she'd greeted him like a…like a lover, he admitted.

He groaned, raking a frustrated hand across the back of his neck. Suddenly, he wanted answers, not more questions. He stood up.

With a letdown feeling, he discovered that her office was empty. She must have left right after he dumped all that accusation and bitterness on her. Left her desk a mess too, he noted, moving slowly toward it. That was unlike her, a pretty good indication of her emotional state, he acknowledged with something very like remorse.

Idly, he flicked at the report folded on top of the desk, wondering whether Petrie had given her much static over accessing the computer system. He noticed that the report wasn't set up like the others.

Casually, he ran down the column of figures, then with more interest, he flipped to the second sheet. In seconds, he sank into Sidney's chair, his attention riveted on the report.

This time there was no misunderstanding! He was reading the one single document that would destroy Rutledge Enterprises.

Chapter Eleven

Gone? But where?"

Gail's eyes did not quite meet Sidney's. "He didn't say, Sidney."

"Well, when will he be back?"

"He didn't say that either, I'm afraid." Gail quickly busied herself shuffling papers on her desk, then whipped off her typewriter cover.

Sidney was beginning to sense that Gail was hedging and she wasn't quite sure why. "Can I know *when* he left, Gail?" she asked patiently.

Embarrassed, Gail gave Sidney an imploring look. "Yesterday, after he discovered—" She bit off whatever it was he'd discovered and jumped up. "Let's get a cup of coffee."

"Sounds good," Sidney murmured thoughtfully. "Let me just get rid of my purse." She turned, heading for her office, one brow raised to see Gail right behind her.

"Sidney—"

At her door, Sidney stopped short. Her desk was cleared off, her office as empty and uninhabited looking as it had been the day she moved in. Puzzled, she pulled open first one drawer, then another. They yielded only a few meager unused supplies. Frowning, she looked around for the report she'd left on the desk after talking with Louis the night before.

"There was a stack of worksheets and a report on my desk," she told Gail. "Do you know where it is?" She went to the file drawers and began opening and closing each one. They were all empty. A frown knitted her fine brows. "That report, Gail," she repeated, intent on her search. "Where is it?"

"I'm not sure." Gail hesitated a second and then, as though making a decision, she said, "I only know Beau took it with him, Sidney. He was absolutely furious when he discovered it. I've never seen him like that."

Sidney ceased what she was doing and straightened slowly. A sense of dismay settled like a stone in her chest. "Beau has the report?"

Gail's look was answer enough.

"Oh, Lord, he'll never understand," Sidney murmured, her expression so distressed that Gail instinctively reached out to touch her. "He'll think I've been here all along not to help him but to destroy him. Oh, Gail, he'll hate me for this!"

Alarmed, Gail began to bustle about, pulling out a chair, gently pushing Sidney down into it. "Now there's no sense in jumping to conclusions," she said calmly, placing a warm hand on Sidney's shoulder. "You can explain first thing when he gets back."

Sidney ran a distracted gaze over the empty office. "It doesn't look like he expects me to be here when he gets back," she said bleakly. "It looks like I've been fired."

"Well, like I said, honey, let's don't jump to conclusions. I'm counting on that man having more horse sense than to believe you would do anything to hurt him."

Sidney's lips curved in a weak smile, warmed by Gail's vote of confidence. But it wasn't Gail whose business was on the line. It was impossible to miss the significance of the cleaned-out desk and empty office. It was clear that Sidney was now persona non grata at Rutledge Enterprises.

What must he have thought when he found that damning report? That she'd sent the Peabody bank the numbers that would ruin him? Of course. Dejectedly, Sidney leaned over and turned the computer on. She activated a few commands, forcing herself to concentrate. He might have taken her worksheets, but he hadn't been able to erase the material she'd stored.

Blankly, she stared at the display before her. After what he'd learned about her yesterday, he probably believed the worse—that she'd sent the report on to the bank. She sighed softly and turned her machine off again. Now what?

"If only I knew what he planned to do," she murmured, her eyes troubled.

"I'm sorry about this, Sidney," Gail said with compassion. "He turned the whole place upside down. Had me call Jim Mason out at the number three mill, then he told Oliver Petrie—"

"Don't tell me, let me guess," Sidney interrupted with a grim smile. "Oliver's entire kingdom is again off limits."

Gail extended her palms helplessly. "More or less."

Sidney rose and went to the door. "Let's get that coffee."

"I collected your personal things and put them in my office," Gail said, passing a cup to Sidney and pouring one for herself.

"Thanks," Sidney returned absently, her mind busy with a new plan. "It's no big deal." She drifted back toward her office, sipping the coffee. "What does matter is finding Beau."

She turned to Gail with a determined look. "Gail, it's absolutely vital that I talk to him today, and the sooner the better. I can't go into detail with you, but if you know where he is, you can save him and the company a lot of grief by telling me."

Gail shook her head. "I don't know, Sidney. He didn't tell me where he was going or how long he'd be gone."

"Okay." Sidney tapped a forefinger against her coffee cup, thinking. He wouldn't disappear from Memphis without telling his mother or Megan where he'd be. She picked up the phone.

"Megan? Sidney here, how are you today, honey?"

"Okay, Sid. Just getting ready for cheerleader practice. My ankle's still too weak for some of the routines, but I can't miss any sessions. Gotta keep in shape for the big try!"

"I know you can do it, Meggie," Sidney said with sincere confidence. "Listen, honey, is Beau home? Could I talk to him?"

Megan hesitated, then said casually, "Uh, gosh, Sid, isn't he there? At the office? Have you asked Gail? She always knows—"

"Megan."

Another short silence.

"Did he mention that I might be calling?" Sidney asked.

Megan cleared her throat. "I think I remember him saying something," she began cautiously.

"Megan, your uncle believes I've done something that will damage his business. I haven't. I'm even hoping to prevent that something from happening, but I need to speak to him to do it." She waited, praying that the bonds of her friendship with Megan were strong enough to overcome Beau's orders. "Please trust me, Megan."

Relief flooded her as Megan said, "He's in Atlanta, Sid."

After thanking Megan, Sidney hung up, her expression thoughtful. Had Beau simply cut his losses and decided to chuck everything? She discarded that idea almost instantly. Had he gone back to Lisa? Hardly. That was equally unlikely. Still, why did he leave? After reading the numbers, he must have known he would be the only person that the bank would look to for an explanation. He might, just might, have talked them into another loan.

Late yesterday when she'd called Louis, she'd requested an extension and he'd granted it. She'd decided not to reveal the fraud perpetrated by Petrie and Trehern to Louis before she told Beau. When Louis had pressed her for a reason for the extension request, she had put him off, promising him she was very close to verifying his original suspicions of wrongdoing at Rutledge. He'd grumbled, but finally had agreed to wait until today.

But Beau's sudden disappearance complicated everything. The problem was that Sidney couldn't stall Louis for very long. She'd planned to tell Beau everything, then go with him to the bank. With Louis's help, it shouldn't be impossible to continue the extension while charges were filed against Petrie and Trehern. A crime had been committed. It was no longer just the bank and Beau's company involved.

She raked a hand through her hair and began pacing her small office. She couldn't call Louis now. Although she had Petrie and Trehern cold, there was no guarantee that Beau wasn't involved. His absence was bound to look suspicious. Until a few days ago, it would have looked suspicious to her. Now she knew him, really knew him. There was a good explanation for his sudden disappearance and it wasn't guilt. But she didn't want to have to sell that to Louis Maynard. Her intercom buzzed.

"Sidney, Mr. Maynard at the bank wants to talk to you."

She glanced at her watch, surprised that he'd waited this long. "Will you tell him I'm...uh, at the dentist, Gail?"

A short silence. "The dentist."

"For Beau's sake, Gail, I'm at the dentist." Before Gail's curiosity could be satisfied, Sidney hung up.

Now what? Louis would be put off only so long. Maybe she could take a lunch hour at some unlikely restaurant, and hope and pray that by then Beau would be back. Her intercom buzzed again.

In a deadpan tone, Gail said, "Please call Mr. Maynard when you get back from the dentist."

"Thank you, Gail."

"Don't mention it," Gail returned dryly.

"And Gail, if Louis calls again, please tell him I'm at lunch. And if he wants to talk to Beau, tell him he's...somewhere on the number three tract. Then if

Beau calls, don't let him talk to Louis. Try to convince him to speak to me first. It's a matter of life and death, Gail!''

Beau stood just outside her office listening as Sidney came up with half a dozen ideas for holding the Peabody bank at bay to save his skin. He closed his eyes for a moment, swallowing hard. Love for her, strong and sure, welled up in him, stealing his breath and banishing the last of his doubts. The pain and anger of last night were wiped out in the bigger discovery that he loved her. He'd never felt as betrayed as when he'd stared at the figures she'd compiled, believing he was seeing the destruction of his business and the death of the fragile emotion that had been growing between them. Thank goodness he'd had the sense to go straight to Louis Maynard.

He pushed the door wide and met her wide wary gaze.

''Beau!'' She sprang up from her desk looking like a doe poised for flight.

He advanced, his eyes holding her captive. ''Sidney.'' His tone was soft, silky. ''Still running interference for me at the Peabody, hmm?''

''Beau, where have you been?'' she cried, stifling a crazy urge to throw herself into his arms.

His half laugh thrummed over her senses. She watched as he closed the door with one foot and then leaned against it, big and...uncertain?

''I've been to the bank, then Atlanta, back to Memphis, then to Louis Maynard's house at six this morning,'' he replied. ''The only place I haven't been is the number three mill, honey.''

''Beau, you couldn't have left at a worse time,'' she began, coming from behind the desk, her face anxious.

A part of her thrilled to the sound of the endearment, but another more urgent need compelled her to have everything out in the open between them. She couldn't take any more hostility from him. "I wanted to see you about some things that I discovered before the next report went to the bank. We have an extension—"

"We have, hmm?" He pushed away from the door and advanced, his topaz eyes anything but hostile.

Sidney halted, eyeing him warily, torn between an impulse to scramble back behind the safety of her desk and a delicious desire to hurl herself into the compelling amber flame.

"I mean, *you* have an extension of time on the report." She hesitated. "Beau, I wanted to explain that report. I know what you thought when you saw it yesterday. But you were already so mad at me over the agency thing—not that I blame you," she went on hurriedly, backing up as he advanced steadily, until she bumped into the edge of her desk. "When you told me how much damage I'd done to your marriage, aiding and abetting Lisa, even though I didn't mean it, I—"

Beau's mouth came down on hers hungrily, and the rest of her confession was lost forever.

He caught her to him and sprawled against the desk, pulling her forcefully between his thighs. Her hands, eloquent and beseeching moments before, fluttered helplessly before settling naturally on his shoulders, going to his head, then tangling in the already ruffled sun-streaked silk of his hair.

"Sidney, Sidney," he groaned, burying his mouth in the soft skin under her ear. "As usual, we're in the wrong place and I want to make love to you."

She wanted the same thing with a passion so fierce that it shocked her. But what had happened to change his mind about her? She pushed against his chest and leaned back seeking his eyes. "I don't understand, Beau," she said, her gaze clouded. "I know I should have told you about my job in Atlanta, but—"

His hands enclosed her waist and, leaning his forehead against hers, he laughed softly. "It took me about twenty minutes yesterday to realize what a damn fool I was to fly off the handle about your job with the Thompson Agency," he admitted, planting a kiss on her nose. "I was out of line, and if it had been anyone else but you, Sidney, I probably wouldn't have overreacted like I did. I know it was nothing personal, that you were just doing a job.

"So I came to your office to talk about it and found that report. I jumped the gun again." His mouth slanted ruefully. "Don't ask me why I thought you would ever try to hurt me, honey. But this time, luck or some remnant of good judgment made me go straight to Louis Maynard." His hands at her waist tightened and she interrupted anxiously.

"But that report was what I wanted to talk to you about, Beau. Oliver Petrie has been practicing some very clever white-collar crime."

"I know."

Her mouth dropped. "You know?"

"Well, I wasn't certain, but I'd been suspicious of him from the first. I decided he'd be more likely to tip his hand if he stayed right where he was. If I'd known of your special penchant for financial sleuthing, sweetheart, I'd have rested a lot easier. As it was, I ran my own numbers every week with the help of a couple of staff people in Petrie's section. After what happened to me in Atlanta, I would have been a fool not to have a system of checks and balances."

She looked at him with new respect. "You mean I worried all this time for nothing?"

He chuckled and hugged her. "Not really. To be honest, the material I found on your desk yesterday was just what I needed to tie Vince Trehern in. I hadn't been able to do that on my own."

"Did Louis know all this?" she asked.

"More or less. I called him to request that he use the bank's resources to run a profile on Trehern and Petrie. Seems they're partners in more than one venture. But he didn't tell me that you were at Rutledge for any reason except tracking the loan. When I told him I thought you believed I was stealing from my own company, he was quick to set me straight. You know what he told me?" Beau said with a catch in his voice.

She stared at him mutely.

"He told me flatly that you didn't suspect me, that you were actually shielding me. He guessed, shrewdly, that because of your expertise in computer fraud, you probably knew exactly what was going on. He said you'd called and asked for an extension, obviously stalling for time. Louis told me he believed you'd already solved the problem but it looked bad for me, so you were reluctant to turn it over to the bank."

Sidney looked at Beau, trying to decide whether or not he resented her "running interference" for him. "How did Louis know I didn't suspect you?"

Beau smiled. "There have been many times when you could have expressed doubt of my integrity to Louis, darling. The weekly reports showed a steady decline in production and I'm certain the material you pulled from the computer must have suggested that somebody was raking it in off the top, yet you never said a word to him."

Sidney managed a look that she hoped was noncommittal, but Beau wasn't fooled. "I had the most opportunity to steal from my company and you had every reason to suspect me after my questionable reputation in Atlanta. And I had certainly thwarted most of your efforts to do anything except track the loan."

He wasn't resentful. There was warmth and tenderness in his eyes. Sidney melted under the fire of that look, burying her face in his shirtfront.

"Most interesting," Beau mused teasingly. "But there's still something I can't figure out, my darling detective."

"What?" she said weakly, shivering when his hands skated up her rib cage and grazed the side of her breasts.

"Why would a practical, down-to-earth accountant such as yourself, with absolutely no proof otherwise, go to bat for a notorious chauvinistic libertine such as me?"

If he only knew. Around Beau she didn't feel practical or down-to-earth. Around him, that crazy capricious streak in her nature took control of her senses and robbed her of all good sense and practicality. Dwelling on the tawny hair at the V of his shirt, she sought for a sensible answer. "I— It was—" She took a deep breath and managed a modicum of dignity. "I simply wanted to present Louis with a complete professional assessment of the situation."

Beau laughed outright. "And you did it too, honey. That was a highly professional job. Thanks to you, I know exactly where I am production-wise, and you produced proof of collusion between Petrie and Trehern." As she glowed from his generous praise, he warmed to the subject. "Actually, you probably plucked Rutledge Enterprises right from the edge of bankruptcy."

She threw him a suspicious look. "Hmm," she murmured dryly, "I guess it's pretty convenient to have a shark at the Peabody in your corner, huh?"

He winced. "I'm sorry I called you a shark."

"Does this mean you no longer think of me as a computer?" she persisted mercilessly, gasping suddenly when he nipped at her neck.

"Computers don't taste like this."

She melted bonelessly against him when his tongue circled the delicate shell of her ear. "Is this the part where I fall at your feet?"

"Uh-huh."

He was kissing her again, and it was heaven. If she lived to be a hundred, she would still adore this man's kisses. She made a little whimper of protest when he abandoned her mouth. His fingers were at the buttons on her blouse. He separated the silk and then his warm breath fanned the sensitive flesh at her breast. A delicious pang rocked her when he caught a nipple between his teeth and gently tugged. "What about your prejudice against a lady with a plan?"

"I love it when a plan comes together."

The surprising thing, Sidney thought helplessly, was that she didn't actually fall in a boneless heap at his feet. And where that thought would have troubled her before, now she gave herself over willingly to the pleasure of knowing that Beau was equally aroused. It was a heady thing, loving a man like Beau Rutledge.

Beau was still suddenly, his eyes dark and golden, intent on hers. "Say that again," he demanded thickly.

"What?"

"About loving me."

She made a little noise and buried her nose in his shirtfront again. It showed the state of her emotions that she had spoken out loud and hadn't even realized it!

He caught her fiery hair in two gentle fists and forced her eyes to his. "Is it true, Sidney? Because I fell in love with you on the stairs of the Peabody Bank, and nothing's been the same since."

She looked amazed, and he gave her a gentle shake. "Don't look so surprised, woman! I did everything in my power to fight it. I had an image in my mind of the ideal woman and she looked just like you. But your career and your life-style didn't fit my ideal. Not that it mattered. The more I saw you, the more I wanted you. I told myself I didn't need another tangle like the one I'd been involved in with Lisa."

"I'm not like Lisa," Sidney said vehemently.

"I know, sweetheart," he said hugging her hard. "I was just too pigheaded to see it. I held out as long as I could, watching you charm everybody you came close to. Megan loved you, my mother loved you, even Gail. I love you!"

Her eyes were wide and very green. "You do?"

"I do." He kissed her with wry tenderness. "And I didn't mean to yell it like that. I was planning lots of champagne and moonlight when I told you."

"No narrow bunks in crew's quarters?"

"No. And the only fire raging out of control will be between us."

"Why did you go to Atlanta?" she said, her cheek against his chest.

He was still for a second. "The assets from my business were tied up when I first left Atlanta," he explained. "But no more. Fortunately, I'm now in a position to infuse some capital into Rutledge Enterprises. So when I thought I might need a lot of money in a hurry, I flew to Atlanta to arrange it. As it turned out, I won't need to do that."

Pushing away, she stared in mingled hope and fear. "You mean Lisa didn't ruin you financially?"

He grinned. "She gave it her best shot, but I'm not as easy to fleece as she thought."

In a burst of love and relief, Sidney hugged him. "Oh, I'm so glad. And so relieved."

It was Beau's turn to push back and catch her eye. "You weren't keen to marry a penniless man?"

Her heart melted. "Is that a proposal?"

"Is that look an answer?"

"I don't care if you haven't got a nickel," she said, passion lacing her husky voice. "I'm just so glad I don't have to feel guilty about contributing to your financial ruin on top of everything else."

He caught her up and kissed her hard. "You aren't to blame for anything that happened to me in Atlanta, Sidney. Lisa and her neurotic ambition were the cause of everything. I'm even beginning to feel obliged to her."

Sidney looked outraged. "How?"

He grinned. "I'm free now to love you, right?"

Mollified, she nuzzled her face against his neck then pressed a fierce little kiss there. "I love you, John Beaufort Rutledge."

His laugh was husky. Beneath her lips, Sidney could feel the pulse throbbing in his throat. "I love you too, sweetheart."

She raised on tiptoe and sought his mouth, sighing as he rained little kisses all over her face, holding her tenderly.

"Will you marry me, darling?"

"Yes, oh yes." She sighed happily, snuggling into his arms.

"And do my income tax every April?"

"Beau!"

He laughed, easily fending off her quick blow. "Okay, okay. Anyway, I have a man who's probably better—"

He stopped at the unmistakable threat in her green eyes.

"—better off without me as a client," he finished, his eyes dancing. He caught her wrists and pinned them both behind her. "Besides, you have talents that are much more interesting than a flair for business."

"That's more like it," she said with satisfaction, snuggling against him like an affectionate kitten. "I'm not worried, I'll soon have all your chauvinistic tendencies subdued."

He rubbed his nose gently up and down against her cheek. "Uh-hmm." He murmured something noncommittal, hiding a wicked glint in his eye. "We're going to get along fine, just as soon as you know your place, little woman."

"Beau!" Exasperated, she gave him a fierce look, her green eyes laughing. "Just out of curiosity, mind you, but where in your opinion is this little woman's place?"

He grinned lazily, his topaz eyes warm and wonderful. "In my life, forever."

The Silhouette Cameo Tote Bag Now available for just $6.99

Handsomely designed in blue and bright pink, its stylish good looks make the Cameo Tote Bag an attractive accessory. The Cameo Tote Bag is big and roomy (13″ square), with reinforced handles and a snap-shut top. You can buy the Cameo Tote Bag for $6.99, plus $1.50 for postage and handling.

Send your name and address with check or money order for $6.99 (plus $1.50 postage and handling), a total of $8.49 to:

**Silhouette Books
120 Brighton Road
P.O. Box 5084
Clifton, NJ 07015-5084
ATTN: Tote Bag**

SIL–T–1R

The Silhouette Cameo Tote Bag can be purchased pre-paid only. No charges will be accepted. Please allow 4 to 6 weeks for delivery.

N.Y. State Residents Please Add Sales Tax

Offer not available in Canada.

READERS' COMMENTS ON
SILHOUETTE ROMANCES:

"I would like to congratulate you on the most wonderful books I've had the pleasure of reading. They are a tremendous joy to those of us who have yet to meet the man of our dreams. From reading your books I quite truly believe that he will someday appear before me like a prince!"
— L.L.*, Hollandale, MS

"Your books are great, wholesome fiction, always with an upbeat, happy ending. Thank you."
— M.D., Massena, NY

"My boyfriend always teases me about Silhouette Books. He asks me, how's my love life and naturally I say terrific, but I tell him that there is always room for a little more romance from Silhouette."
— F.N., Ontario, Canada

"I would like to sincerely express my gratitude to you and your staff for bringing the pleasure of your publications to my attention. Your books are well written, mature and very contemporary."
— D.D., Staten Island, NY

*names available on request

FOUR UNIQUE SERIES
FOR EVERY WOMAN YOU ARE...

Silhouette Romance

Heartwarming romances that will make you laugh and cry as they bring you all the wonder and magic of falling in love.

6 titles per month

Silhouette Special Edition

Expanded romances written with emotion and heightened romantic tension to ensure powerful stories. A rare blend of passion and dramatic realism.

6 titles per month

Silhouette Desire

Believable, sensuous, compelling—and above all, romantic—these stories deliver the promise of love, the guarantee of satisfaction.

6 titles per month

Silhouette Intimate Moments

Love stories that entice; longer, more sensuous romances filled with adventure, suspense, glamour and melodrama.

4 titles per month

Silhouette Romances
not available in retail outlets in Canada

SIL-GEN-1A